The White Chiffon SARI

The White Chiffon SARI

A collection of short stories
By Mithra Venkatraj

Translated from Kannada
By Venkatraja U. Rao

PARTRIDGE
A Penguin Random House Company

To order additional copies of this book, contact
Partridge India
000 800 10062 62
www.partridgepublishing.com/india
orders.india@partridgepublishing.com

CONTENTS

ABOUT THE AUTHOR

Mithra Venkatraj grew up in Kundapura, a town by the sea in coastal Karnataka. After her marriage (to Venkatraja Rao), she moved to Mumbai where she now lives.

Mithra began to write fiction while she was still in college in her native town, but it was in Mumbai that she did most of her writing.

Mithra Venkatraj is an important short story writer in Kannada, and with her maiden novel published recently, she has received instant recognition as a significant novelist as well. She has published 3 short story collections and a novel so far, which have won her several major literary awards.

Her short stories have been included in definitive anthologies and some have been translated into English, and one of them won her the 'Katha' award in 1993.

Mithra writes subtly and movingly about human relations in all its diversity, exploring its frailties and triumphs with great empathy and understanding. Finely etched characters, a touch of humour, a sharp eye for details and evocative capture of the milieu—make her writings stand out.

THE WHITE CHIFFON SARI

I remember my mother saying that Inasa Nayaka's wife, Katribai, wouldn't have died so early if at least one of her three daughters had got married during her lifetime.

Inasa Nayaka's was the very first house east of ours, in an area known as 'Nayaka colony'.

When I was old enough to run around and became a very frisky little boy, there were many occasions for my mother to either try and keep me away from mischief or placate me when I kept crying stubbornly, and on those occasions, it was likely that I'd be seated on our compound wall to be shown the cute little chicks that ran around in the adjoining Inasa compound. I would delight in watching them moving around on their tiny legs, pecking at the ground while hurrying every once in a while to catch up with the mother hen leading them. When the chicks were too small, they would be confined to the coop for fear of being lifted by a kite or a crow, but no sooner one of

1

Katribai's daughters—Rosy or Pillu—saw me perched on the wall than they would pick some chicks from the coop, bring them to me, and sidling up to the wall, display them on their spread out palms to my utter delight.

Inasa Nayaka's house was small with thatched roof. On the narrow porch of their house which was open—except during rainy season when woven dry palm-fronds covered it—a wooden bench and a table could be seen from our house. A couple of steps up from the porch was a living room and then a small kitchen—apparently that was all to that house. Directly outside the kitchen in the yard, Katribai or one of her daughters would sometimes be seen cutting fish for cooking.

Katribai's eldest daughter, Jennybai, after passing the eighth standard government examination and getting trained as a teacher, was teaching in an elementary school in Hejamadi, about five miles from our town. Since it was tedious to travel up and down, she had rented a room near her school and visited her parents' house once in a week or two. Katribai would say that somebody had to work after all to take care of the family's expenses.

Inasa Nayaka did not have any earnings to speak of. He was an easy going, small-time tailor who sat in the clutter of a cloth shop, doing more chit-chatting and less earning. And when he did earn some money, he never committed the sin of spending it on his family or sharing it with Katribai, but spent it on liquor to get sloshed. Later he would be seen walking home at some unearthly hour, weaving in and out unsteadily, and making an unholy drunken racket that woke up whole neighbourhoods. And hearing his loud voice from a distance, Katribai and her daughters would turn off the lights, spread their mattresses and quietly go to bed so as to avoid any confrontation with him. If the daughters grumbled about his ways to their mother, they would be silenced by Katribai's cutting remark about her husband, 'to hell with his money . . . and let him do whatever he wants with it'.

Being home for weekends, the eldest daughter Jennybai would sometimes have arguments with her father in the nights when he returned home drunk—which could be clearly heard by us in the quiet of the night. Her fights could perhaps be justified as the righteous indignation of an earning member of the family—but it always ended the same way—with Inasa Nayaka screaming, then the din of the dishes being thrown, and finally the loud voices of his daughters countering him. Such commotion meant that we wouldn't be hearing the high pitched and, what was to our ears, off-key singing of Christian hymns by the three sisters of Inasa-family that night.

On other days, since we too sang our devotional 'bhajan-songs' at about the same time in the late evenings, but at a lower key, the two music streams appeared to be on collision course. Anyway, I used to easily get tired of our singing, as with anything that I felt was long drawn, and would drift off to the dining room to stand near the window from where I could listen to the singing from Inasa household. With the cadence of their singing rising ever so high, as if trying to reach the heaven itself, and then plunging precipitously, it perhaps sounded more interesting than our music sung to precise and predictable beat.

3

What I remember best is that when their singing reached its high point, it was mostly Rosy's voice that seemed to dominate with its clarity. My mother used to say that when Rosy was not home, their music lacked its gusto, and on those days, I remember just a couple of songs being sung with abrupt halts, broken voices and a final collapse into an off-key ending.

When Inasa got drunk and came home tottering on his feet, the road was like a stage for him to perform. He would holler like he was addressing a crowd, waking up the houses that lined the road. When he appeared before our house, he would stop to hail my doctor-father by lifting both his hands above his head and joining them to say, "Doctor, here's a big salutation to you" and then acclaim, "Our Doctor is a good man, there is none like him in this town—in this country—I'd say in the whole world!" Such hailing would continue as we peeped through the latticed window and fretted what other pearls of wisdom might fall from Inasa's lips. My father would peep from the window of his clinic and without a trace of hesitation shout, "Get lost, Inasa! That's enough" Sometimes he would summon our servant and say, "Manja, Chase that fellow away" and Manja would forthwith put an end to Inasa's grandstanding.

At times when Inasa's intoxication level reached new peaks, his drunken babble during his customary stop in front of our house would include a wholly unnecessary declaration, "If only this good Doctor orders me to fix anybody . . . count on me to fix that fellow in no time"

But this very same Inasa, sounding so brave when drunk, was meek as a lamb when sober, and hesitated as much as to raise his head in the presence of my father let alone open his mouth to speak.

Sometimes, when Inasa had a very bad hangover in the mornings, Rosy or Pillu would appear at the wall separating our two compounds to ask my mother for buttermilk, which was supposed to be a cure for it. My mother would then fill a jug with buttermilk—not forgetting to drop a piece of dry red chilli into it against the casting of any evil eye on our cattle—and hand it across the wall. Most exchanges between our two houses took place across the compound wall. One such exchange was of our over-spicy '*saru*', which went very well with rice. It was known as 'Brahmin-*saru*' in the territory across the wall where it was a much desired food item. Another was our pickle, much coveted by Katribai. In fact, mother used to recall that Katribai had our pickle for her very last meal of her life.

Each of Katribai's three daughters was different. Looking at Jennybai,—with her rough, heavily acned face and hair tied into a bun so tight that no strand of hair was free—I felt she had never been young in her life. Her Kannada was clear like a teacher's, and it reminded me so strongly of school that I felt ill at ease in her presence.

Jennybai had passed the age of marriage and did not seem to spare any further thoughts to it. Well, who knows, she might as well be hiding those thoughts somewhere inside her. If someone did ask about it, she would say, crossing herself, 'Marriage for me did you say . . . Only in the next world . . . !'

But I had heard Jennybai telling my mother, 'Who is going to feed them if I get married? The house has to run somehow' and she had ended by saying, 'Presently my concern is Rosy and I am looking for a husband for her.'

Jennybai used to derive great satisfaction in recounting the hard work and efforts she was putting in to support her family. She often complained how her two sisters were so blasé about the great sacrifices she was making for the family and how bad were their behaviour and actions. Of course, it had to be admitted that it was only because of Jennybai that the family could have food on its plates.

All of us in our house believed that Rosy was the best looking among the Inasa-daughters; not just because she was slender and fair, but also because she was charming and attractive. She had an oval face, rounded forehead, full cheeks and strikingly dark eyes. On her right cheek, a little away from her nose was a black mole. Rosy used to remember that, when I was a child and being held in her arms, I would always try to pluck that mole. She had told me this so many times that it has stayed in my mind as my own memory.

Pillu, the last one, was a spitting image of her father, with a face square and wide, and a body that was short and plump.

Rosy and Pillu rarely wore saris; they wore skirts with the hemline just below the knee, and blouses that came well below their waists. When the slender Rosy walked, the skirt swirled, swished and swayed. We had noted that Rosy's attire changed when a suitor was expected to visit. She would, in that case, wear a neatly draped sari and sit on the bench in their porch, waiting.

The impending visit of any suitor was a very hush-hush affair in Inasa household, but there were plenty of indications for those who were curious. A chair being borrowed from Kamthi's house, a request to my mother to lend the lacy table cloth or for that matter Rosy wearing sari—all these were sure to make the neighbourhood rife with speculations. And our maid Anthi would be the very 'cocoon of curiosity'. She would keep a diligent eye on the Inasa compound even as she washed our clothes on the platform of our well. No sooner she saw the visitors enter the gate of the Inasa-compound than Anthi would be all winking eyes.

Part of the porch of Inasa's house was directly visible from the platform of our well and all my sisters would collect there, overwhelmingly curious to see Rosy's future husband. I too would try to squeeze my way into that crowd but would be rebuffed and often expelled with intolerant remarks like—'what business does this little kid have here? He wants to be here just because everyone else is here!'

When I was very small, the Inasa-girls were very fond of me. They had no boys in their house, while in our house I was the only boy and the darling of the entire family. I faintly remember that when the Inasa-sisters visited our house, they would hold me and squeeze me with great affection. But I would wriggle out of their hold and get away, greatly annoying them and making them complain to my mother, 'Look, Amma! He runs away . . . and all that we want is to show some affection'. And, 'All they wanted' was to hold and squeeze me in their arms and then pinch and kiss my cheeks till they hurt. But I just disliked being restrained and held in anybody's arms. I was a very frisky kid and didn't tolerate even a momentary constraint to my movement.

When I grew to be about three or four years old, their love and affection took on the form of teasing me endlessly. No sooner their eyes fell on me than they would start making fun of me or close in on me from all sides, crying 'Catch him, catch him—don't let him get away' But the worst was when their visit coincided with my mother choosing to dress me up in the porch. She would be holding my shorts in her hands for me to step into them and the girls would have just stepped into the porch.

Upon noticing that I have nothing on me, they would start giggling uncontrollably and cheering wildly, 'Look! Look! Look at him!'

Getting confused I would try to run away but my mother would hold my hand tight and won't let me go, even as she got into small talk with the girls. Pretending to catch me, they'd cry, 'He is so . . . shy . . . Catch him before he runs'

I wouldn't understand their idea of fun and would get terribly offended, while it wouldn't occur to my mother to protect my modesty or show me any mercy. She would neither let me get away nor be in a hurry to make me wear my shorts. She would hold it distractedly and say to my utter annoyance, 'What's wrong with this kid? Come on, let me put on the shorts. Why! Such a small kid but so shy! Come, come. Why make such a fuss?' and to my mortification, she would add, 'they have seen it all anyway when you were a baby.'

I would be furious—just because they have seen me like that at one time, do they get the license to see me like that for ever?

It was just about the time I had started going to school I think, when one day my mother asked Rosy some question—I don't remember what it was, but my guess would be that it was about her marriage, a question that was invariably asked whenever Rosy visited us—and she had begun to say with resignation, 'I don't want any marriage and I don't want any husband'—but then her eyes fell on me and suddenly she giggled as if an amusing thought occurred to her, and she declared, 'I wouldn't mind him as my husband, what do you say, my boy?'

That was the day my real troubles started. From that day onwards, any time and for no rhyme or reason, I began to be called and addressed as 'Rosy's husband'.

Though I had no idea what a husband was, the way it was said and the laughter that came with it were enough for me to know that I was being made fun of.

No sooner Rosy neared our gate, than my sisters would start giggling and cheering 'Look, your wife has come! Look, your wife is here!' And as for Rosy, she would start inquiring with great fanfare as she stepped into our house, 'Where is my hubby?'

Utterly embarrassed, I would vanish into the house and dodge her till she left. Even if I continued to be in her presence, I would make a long face and pretend to be unconcerned and busy—playing or scribbling on my slate—and Rosy would start, 'Oh! I am afraid my husband is angry with me,'

Sometimes I would shout at Rosy, 'GO AWAY! I am not your husband' and bolt from there. But that didn't work well because it seemed to cause even greater mirth with everyone roaring with laughter behind me.

But I have got to admit that whenever Rosy visited us, from the time she came in, I would wait eagerly for Rosy to call me as her husband, howsoever much was my annoyance with that. With the corner of my eyes on her, I would eagerly wait for that moment; it was the sweet anticipation of a dreaded moment. Rosy, lost in her worries, would sometimes forget to say and, for some reason unknown to me, it would leave me disaffected and feeling lost. However, as soon as she called me her husband, I would get terribly infuriated as usual, without fail.

After Katribai's passing away, Inasa's health began to fail and gradually he stopped going to the shop. He then began to work the sewing machine at home. But he was more often found lying at home in drunken stupor than sewing on the machine. The girls started using his machine; more for repair work than for new clothing, and that too mostly to oblige neighbours, including my mother who gave them her torn petty coats or blouses with missing hooks for repair.

One Sunday, while on the road returning from Church, Jennybai was seen yelling at her sisters—mostly at Rosy—and even hitting her on her back or knuckle-knocking on her head. The whole neighbourhood could hear her accusing Rosy of winking at a boy while praying in the church.

When she was with my mother, Jennybai would always talk about her responsibilities, that is, the ones she had taken upon herself. She complained how hard it was for her to support the family, how irresponsible and insensible were her sisters—wandering the streets or visiting friends endlessly—and what little chance was there for any good marriage proposal to crop up for them in the circumstances. The litany would go on.

Mother would try to console Jennybai by being positive about the prospects of her sisters' marriage, but in return, Jennybai would say that her hair had gone grey just by running around in the sun chasing marriage proposals for her sisters with no results at all to show for it.

It was, of course, a fact that Jennybai's hair had become grey and my mother and my aunt who was staying with us those days, were greatly sympathetic to her on account of that.

In general, whether neighbours or relatives, they all had sympathy and admiration for Jennybai for the efforts she was putting in for the marriage of her sisters, but at the same time they had only disapproval for her 'wayward' sisters.

It was a custom of Inasa's family to set up a temporary outdoor bath every summer. A hearth would be made in a corner of the compound over which a cauldron kept for warming the water for bath, and covered on all sides with woven dry fronds of coconut tree—leaving the top open. We could see the vapours rising from the open top of this makeshift bath when the sisters had their grand baths every Saturday. One such Saturday, Rosy had been seen going around in the yard, fresh after taking bath, drying her luxurious hair which cascaded behind her in wavy splendour. All of a sudden, Jennybai had descended on her ferociously, hitting and admonishing her, and finally dragging her by her hair into the house.

Around this time Jenny was used to saying that she was getting utterly tired of going around in the heat of the Saturday afternoons, that too, right after weeklong slogging in the school, to chase the marriage proposals that came for her sisters. She complained to my mother, 'And you think they'd agree to the proposals easily? Far from it . . . . No boy is right for them—this one is too thin . . . the other one too fat, this one's job is lowly, other's nose is funny . . . and that fellow is surely a drunkard . . . so on and on!'

After the commotion of Saturday, when Rosy and Pillu visited us, my mother tried to give them some advice, 'Why do you girls harass your sister? She is doing so much to arrange marriages for you! Your mother too is no more . . .' and she went on in this vein.

Pillu interjected, 'Seethamma, you don't know anything! What does she do exactly? Is she trying to find marriage proposals for us or wrecking those which are really good?'

Mother was surprised.

By then Rosy interrupted her sister, 'Stop it Pillu . . . Why bother her with all our irrelevant tales?' but she was overcome with emotion and turned her face away.

Then, saying, 'Come on let's go, Pillu' she abruptly got up and left. I was then playing with a ball in the yard. I stopped playing and stood watching Rosy as she walked past me wiping her tears.

'I believe the proposal from Barkur was good, but I was told that you two rejected it outright' mother said in the manner of questioning.

Pillu answered spiritedly, 'If I said anything it would only shame us. Do you know the age of that suitor from Barkur? He is so old that he has children who themselves are ready for marriage! When Rosy said in a huff, 'Why not I remain a spinster instead of marrying that old man?' Jenny got furious and pulled Rosy by her and hit her. I could go on like this—but I don't wish to shame her, that's all'

Pillu continued, lowering her voice, 'I don't know what's with Jenny. When everything falls in place for a good marriage alliance, she would say something wrong and then it is all over! Just see, only a couple of months ago, son of Fernandez . . . . the owner of the textile shop in Brahmavar . . . . he got very interested in Rosy after seeing her in the church. You know his parents visited us later asking for Rosy's hand for their son. But Jenny didn't like the idea . . . she started rebuking Rosy instead—what did you do in the church? Do you go to for praying or for dallying?—and the way she abused her was shameful.' Pillu had shuddered remembering that painful episode.

My mother asked, 'what happened finally?'

'What could possibly have happened?' Pillu asked rhetorically, adding, 'You wouldn't believe if I told you the truth. Honestly, I can't bring myself to tell the awful truth'

By then I had gone between them to pick the ball I was playing with, and was roundly scolded for that act by my mother, 'Go away kid. You have no business here.'

Pillu whispered in my mother's ear, 'we strongly suspect that she wrote an anonymous poison letter to Fernandez against Rosy. But for heaven's sake, please keep it to yourself. If ever Rosy comes to know that I have told you about it, she will not spare a single bone in my body.'

When Rosy's marriage was finally fixed, I was perhaps the one most relieved. I thought—no more teasing about being a 'husband' at every turn. I remember I was in the fourth standard at that time.

Rosy's wedding took place in the church and the wedding procession went past our house. As the procession neared our house and I heard the clang of the cymbals, I was instantly alerted by it. I had screamed with great excitement for the benefit of my family, 'It is Rosy's wedding band!'

My sisters, mother, my aunt, the servants—everyone except my father—were at the gate in no time at all to watch the procession. I climbed on top of one of the gate posts for a commanding view. Inasa, who had not been well for months, was in the front of the procession and was even making some attempt at dancing with others by throwing his legs and flaying his arms randomly. His movements suggested that he had not deprived himself of his daily quota of liquor, as pointed out to my mother by one of my aunts.

The bride was wearing a white chiffon sari. With pleats spreading out and reaching down to her feet, it appeared as if Rosy was floating down the street in the white cloud of a sari. From behind the diaphanous veil that she wore, I got the feeling that she smiled at me. She had threaded her arm through that of the groom who was fully suited and booted.

I did not go to the wedding dinner. My mother chose to take only my sisters, prejudging me for possible misdemeanours like impatience, fidgeting and straying off, with the final verdict that, 'it will be impossible to keep an eye on him.' It was not a fair trial and I sulked after they left me, feeling cheated. But I did not waste much time. I got easily engaged with a few centipedes crawling in the yard. Idea was to provoke them with twigs to coil themselves so that the same twigs could be threaded through their centres to hold them up for display. After completing that job, I got on a tree and busied myself diverting a line of red ants from their leafy nests—and that was just for the fun of it.

In the aftermath of Rosy's wedding the comments about Rosy's husband were favourable—'not bad, he is okay' 'he is good looking . . . has a job . . . . Made for Rosy'—that sort of thing.

But I had not observed him properly in the wedding procession, for my attention was more on the lively band in the lead with its white drums, the brass cymbals shining bright, the coiled trumpets looking as if ready to spring, the clarinet with its many knobs and buttons and the colourful uniforms of the performers . . . . I was so totally absorbed in the band that the groom had obviously escaped my scrutiny.

Rosy moved into her husband's house in Koteshwara after her marriage. The family was engaged in cultivation and Rosy was kept busy all the time. Her husband, who was all suit and boot in the wedding procession, was actually a fitter in an auto-repair garage in Hanglur.

Apparently, Rosy's life in her husband's house was not easy.

Pillu sympathized with Rosy,—'Poor thing, she has too much work',—but Jennybai countered, 'Husband's house means work, and more work. Here she was wandering all over the town and was not used to bend her back . . . she'll get used to. She'll be all right'

Rosy visited us a couple of times after her marriage and met my mother and others, but I missed her during those visits. I was then in the fifth standard and my world had expanded, and I did not spend much time with my sisters or mother like in the earlier days.

Once I overheard my aunt saying, 'Rosy came to day. She has become very thin. She appeared to be pregnant.'

It came to be known through Pillu that Rosy's husband was a heavy drinker.

Later we found out that it was known before the marriage that Rosy's husband was a habitual drinker, and also that Jennybai had brushed aside Rosy's concern, saying, 'Why make such a fuss about drinking? What does she lose if her husband drinks a little? Is there anybody in our catholic community who doesn't?'

One day, as I was returning from school, I saw Rosy in the bustle of the crowded market place. I couldn't recognize her at first. She and her sister Pillu were buying vegetables. I saw Pillu poke Rosy's side, laughing big, to draw her attention to me. I heard Pillu say to Rosy, "Look, your ex-husband!'

Rosy did not have her hair in a plait like in earlier days; she had tied it into a tight bun. Instead of the usual skirt and blouse, she was wearing a sari.

This Rosy invoked an entirely different set of feelings in me.

Her black eyes seemed to have slightly lost their lustre and I discerned something like sorrow in them. The mole on her cheek right below her eye, which I had supposedly tried to pluck at one time as a child, was not briefly visible till I realized that the darkish patch below her eye had submerged it.

Rosy, made aware of me by Pillu, calling me by my pet name, said, 'Hey Putta, don't you remember me?'

Recognizing me, her eyes had lighted up and regained their sparkle.

'Aren't you Rosy' I replied shyly.

Given my adolescence, I was now tall and gangly, and in addition I had a fuzzy moustache and my voice had cracked. I realized Rosy would have had difficulty in recognizing me. I felt embarrassed being a transient stranger to her. Feeling self-conscious in her presence, I couldn't talk to her any further. To my surprise, I just hung my head and walked away without much ado.

I was in the tenth class then, and in such a state of mind that—as my mother complained—was often unaware of things that happened at home, right under my nose, so to say. I was caught in the pressure of studies, as well as of many opposing pulls and pushes. I had by now a large number of friends who took up much of my time and thoughts. I had to also contend with habits and influences that had grown up with me in the recent past,—mainly to do with girls, both real and imaginary, who haunted my thoughts and fantasies while tormenting me by not providing real companionship. All these had got my feelings mixed up and made me rather dreamy and detached.

Rosy sometimes used to figure in the talks at home and some of it did fall on my ears despite my being not particularly attentive—the callousness of her husband's people, the incident of Rosy being made to stand in the rain by her husband as a punishment, her poor health in the recent past and her visits to my father for treatment every time she came to her parents' house, her sister Pillu now saying that she didn't want to marry at all, and things like that. But those were the days when I was so obsessed with our car and driving that much of what I heard did not register in my mind properly.

In those days, we had an elderly man as a driver for our car, who looked dignified and avuncular, and we kids addressed him as 'Uncle Shenoy' out of respect. I loved to accompany him to the garage for any repair or maintenance work, and if it was a weekend when the car had to be taken for repairs, I would exult since I could go with Uncle Shenoy without my school coming in the way. I would, of course, perfunctorily seek permission from my father or mother before jumping into the car to accompany our driver to the garage. Though hard to believe, it was during such trips to the garage that I learnt to drive without my family coming to know of it. Because of that, I could begin to drive no sooner than I attained the age of eighteen and got the permission to drive. This had surprised my people, who wondered how on earth I was able to drive so well without first learning to drive.

Be that as it may, it was about this time that an incident happened which earned me the approbation of my father. The car engine had blown the gasket and, since the garage in our town was unable to fix it, our driver had to take the car to Hanglur, a town at some distance from ours. I was excited at the prospects of, what was to me, a long drive and persuaded our driver to take me along.

Stopping the car in front of the garage, Uncle Shenoy got off muttering, 'Wonder if Pinto is in there or lying somewhere drunk' and walked into the garage calling out 'Pinto . . . Pinto . . . . '.

I followed him and noticed a face popping up from behind the bonnet of a car and answering Uncle Shenoy sharply, 'you'll have to wait, man'.

Undeterred Uncle Shenoy said, 'Pinto, it is urgent. I got to have it for the Doctor's evening visits'

'Not possible! And I don't care about your urgency'

I was surprised by the rudeness of the man. I had not seen anyone talking to Uncle Shenoy so disrespectfully.

Uncle Shenoy said evenly, 'Remember, the Doctor had informed in advance. There is no need to talk crossly.'

'How do you think I should talk? Have you come here to teach me to talk?' said the man laughing derisively as he walked to the back of the garage. The man's rudeness seemed to be incurable.

Uncle Shenoy said to me in a low voice as the man moved away, 'He is our Rosy's husband'

I understood whom he meant, but asked him anyway involuntarily, 'Who?'

'Inasa's . . . .' he began to say, but stopped when he saw the man coming back.

Pinto said to Uncle Shenoy insolently, wiping his hands with a dirty rag, 'Now. What's your problem?' as he walked towards us with a scowl on his face making it overly obvious that Uncle Shenoy was being an utter nuisance for him.

On top of his insolence,—he had addressed Uncle Shenoy in the familiar term for 'you' in Kannada rather than the respectful alternative meant for elders and superiors. I could not imagine Uncle Shenoy being addressed insolently and disrespectfully by anybody, let alone by a car-mechanic in blackened dress and grease covered face and hands. Even my father addressed him respectfully; Uncle Shenoy's character and personality were such. And this man was treating him like trash.

Just like that, I took two steps forward when Pinto neared us, and shoving him, said, 'Who do you think you are, acting so superior. Can't you show some respect to Uncle Shenoy?'

I was unaware that by then I was pulling him by his shirt collar and shaking him up. I had pulled too strongly apparently, for his shirt front got totally torn vertically down. I was baffled by my own behaviour. Never had I exhibited such temper at home, school or college or anywhere else, for that matter. Uncle Shenoy was shocked and stunned by my most unbecoming conduct. But he soon recovered, and holding me back, made me let go of Pinto's shirt. But for his strong intervention, next thing I would probably have done was to hit Pinto hard.

When I reached home, I found that there was no necessity for Uncle Shenoy to brief my father about the incident at the garage. News travelled in our town as if borne on wings. The incident of 'The Doctor's son assaulting a garage-mechanic' had taken on many sinister shapes and reached our home much ahead of us. Even as I was going up the steps to the porch, I had to face my father's angry outbursts, strident advises and taunts, all meant to make me feel ashamed of my recent behaviour. Once I went inside the house, advises and rebukes came from my mother and aunts, and sneers from my sisters.

My aunt asked me in anguish, 'Tell me why you had to join issues with an unworthy fellow like him?'

Greatly agitated by all the admonitions directed at me, I snapped 'Didn't you tell me he hits Rosy and makes her stand in the rain?'

It came out of me just like that.

For a moment they were puzzled, and then were stunned as they realized that the person I had manhandled was actually Rosy's husband.

It was my aunt again who said, 'What does it mean? Are you a judge dispensing judgements? Tell me please, how is it your concern, and what is the connection with the car anyway?' Confused, she left me muttering something to herself, while I pondered on my action.

I remembered the image of Rosy standing in the yard all alone in the pouring rain, dripping wet and shivering, as if I had witnessed the scene myself. Actually, I had only heard my mother and aunt recount the time when Rosy had contracted pneumonia due to that punishment. My father, who had treated her, later remarked that her survival was due to sheer luck. Rosy was cared for by her sisters with whom she had stayed during the recovery. I had heard that, gaunt and frail, Rosy had come to thank my father before leaving for her husband's house. Right behind her was Inasa Nayaka, who said, with folded hands, 'Doctor Sir, you have saved my daughter.'

My father advised her that she should in future avoid exposing herself to cold. This incident concerning Rosy was related so many times and on so many different occasions in our house that I would have got fixated on it I suppose.

After about two years I left my home town for Varanasi to study engineering. That year was perhaps the toughest year of my life till then. Of course, I left with the joy of having got admission in a prestigious university and the excitement of entering a new world; both tempered with the misery of leaving home. My passage through the Benares University was bumpy to begin with—I virtually ran back home from there, being unable to withstand the pressure of adjusting to the new environs and the ragging of my seniors.

But I was persuaded to return to the University after some of my difficulties were resolved and anxieties allayed. One day before I was to return to Varanasi, Rosy visited us. I was in my room, lying on the bed desultorily when I heard her voice. I was not at that time in a mood to see anyone. So I did not go out to meet her. My mother and she were talking and I could hear the low murmur of their conversation. But to my unease, my mother accompanied by Rosy came into my room. I was lying with my face turned away from the door, and I did not turn to greet Rosy.

Rosy said to me, 'Your mother has told me everything. Don't you worry, Raghu. Those kids have no sense. Be brave . . . things will work out, and I'll pray for you.'

Her voice somehow made me feel reassured. But I remained silent.

Mother thrust a packet into my suitcase, saying, 'Rosy brought it for you' and I was told that it contained cashew nuts from her home and that Rosy had roasted them for me.

Next four years of mine were spent in Varanasi except for vacations when I rarely spent time at home, being mostly with friends—playing cricket, swimming and generally hanging out with them. I don't think I ever met Rosy during those days, though I heard her being spoken about in our house—among other things that—she was now a mother of four or five kids and that her husband's people wouldn't allow operation for stopping further births.

It was intriguing that in so many years of my adulthood, although I saw Rosy quite a few times, every time it was that she could recognize me but I could not recognize her. Was it that she used to change so much or was it my poor memory?—I wondered.

Once, just before my wedding, I and my sister were in the porch busy writing addresses of invitees on the envelopes of my wedding invitations. I saw a woman in our courtyard walking towards the porch of my father's clinic which was rather an extension of the porch we were sitting in.

I said to my sister, "someone is coming and she looks rather familiar'

My sister looked up and laughed, 'Hey, you dumb, don't you know, it is Rosy'

It was difficult to reconcile the Rosy I saw with the Rosy I knew—attractive, slender and fair.

She was now in the porch of the clinic and sat on the bench kept there for the patients.

I remember telling my sister then that Rosy had changed—become plump and it appeared that her face had coarsened and eyes somewhat sunken.

My sister had countered me, 'Is it news that she had become plump? Right from the day of her marriage she has been adding weight. She is never well, the poor thing. She takes medicine for asthma that makes her face swell.'

I could see from where I sat that her face had some dark blotches too.

After seeing my father she came to meet me having heard about my wedding.

'What is the name of the princess?' she asked me.

I gave my answers surrounded by the piles of envelopes containing invitation cards.

By then my mother had brought her a glass of drinking water, and with it, Rosy swallowed the pills my father had just dispensed to her.

'He was such a little boy till the other day and now he talks of his wedding!' she said laughing.

My sisters showed her my bride's photo as well as the saris and dresses purchased for the wedding.

While my mother was trying to extract Rosy's promise to attend my wedding, I made an invitation in her name, and went over and handed it to her.

Rosy did not attend the wedding but did come with her children to the feast held next day at our house for the bride's people. I had introduced Rosy to my wife, Suma, that day. But Suma got much of the information about Rosy from my aunt whom we met a few months after our wedding in Bangalore. She was now living there with her son, and had not attended my wedding, being too feeble. She had grown quite old, but that did not in any way affect her memory or her capacity to talk. She seemingly recounted my childhood in its entirety for the benefit of my wife. As my aunt reeled off my stories that naturally included big chunks about Rosy's erstwhile claim on me as her husband, Suma was laughing her head off, while I sat with a forced grin on my face, wondering how come I never knew that Suma could laugh so much and so loud.

During a recent visit to our hometown, Suma and I were walking to the river front one evening, with my one year old son in my arms. On the way we saw Rosy coming towards us at a distance. She was walking with a cloth bag in her hand, slightly swaying form side to side as if very tired. I couldn't recognize her at all and ironically it was Suma who recognized her, though the only time she had met her was at the time of our wedding.

She took me to task, 'How could you not, Raghu?!'

When Rosy heared us she perked up and her face brightened. The first thing she did was to take my child in her arms, saying excitedly, 'Oh my god, it seems like yesterday that I used to take little Raghu in my arms. Isn't it a wonder?'

And when my son tried to pinch the mole on her face, laughing heartily, she exclaimed, 'Now this is surely Raghu's son!'

After leaving Rosy we proceeded to the river front and I replied to Suma's pending question, 'She must have changed a lot; otherwise I would have recognized her'

Suma was surprised. 'Why, she is the same' she countered.

'You have not seen her before' I said.

'Didn't I see her at the time of our wedding three years ago? I remembered her well' replied Suma looking at me, as if she could not understand my strange inability to recognize Rosy.

I fell silent.

I suddenly realized that any time I remembered Rosy or heard about her, for some reason, the only image that came before my mind's eyes was of Rosy in white chiffon sari, floating down the street in the wedding procession, smiling radiantly. It seemed as if all other memories of meeting her later have just evaporated leaving nothing in their place.

'TELL ME A STORY, PARAKKA'

Ambe, all of twelve, sat tidily cross-legged on the floor, twisting her braid with her hand and looking intently at Parakka with her saucer eyes in acute anticipation of Parakka starting off with a story.

"Parakka . . . ! You said you would tell us the 'Story of the Coach'. That's what we want!" the children had clamoured in unison, and Parakka had yielded.

"It is a very old story. I wasn't even born then!' She intoned.

"But mind you, this is a true story. Happened in this very house." she said gravely of what was to come.

"It's the story of the younger brother of your great, great Grandpa,—known as 'Bhīma of the Coach.' He was a giant of a man. Looked just like Bhimasena himself of the Epic."

Just then, Ambe, still saucer-eyed, shot off an innocent question, "Parakka, have you seen Bhimasena?"

Parakka said tersely, "I won't proceed if you ask irrelevant questions in the middle . . . I'd tell only if you'd listen quietly!"

Children hankered for Parakka's stories unmindful of hunger and sleep and Parakka could easily weave a fictional story as she could narrate a real one to keep them hooked.

Parakka, lean and fair, had the habit of stretching her legs in front of her when she sat on the floor to tell a story, while the children, sitting around her with eyes wide open, listened transfixed as if she had cast a spell on them.

The giant Bhīma's description was unfolding,— chest as wide as the front door, long and bushy moustache, all conquering, powerful eyes and a booming voice that went with his mighty body. It was said that if he roared from inside the house, those at the end of the large field in front of the house would tremble and cringe with fear.

In the mornings, after he had downed a bucket of milk, Bhīma would get into the training-room adjoining the front hall for an hour or two of vigorous physical exercises. His huge, muscular body would then be massaged with oil, and they said it needed four masseurs to do that.

Parakka's graphic description made the characters of her story spring to life for the children.

The effect of the scary stories she told was so powerful and lasting that situations often arose when, even in broad daylight, children would be too afraid to go alone from one room to another in that vast house.

Even to step out of the lower veranda to the toilet in the outhouse, or from the dining hall to the central hall,— they ended up needing an escort.

When, prompted by one of the stories, Ambe had gone up to the floor above the entrance hall and looked at the array of weapons such as swords, guns and shields hung on the wall, she was suddenly seized with an utter fear that somebody was behind her back. But she did not dare to turn her head even as her mouth went dry. Her voice got so stuck in the throat that she could not even scream for help. Finally she managed to scamper down the stairs, ran to her Grandma, and burying her face in the folds of her sari, whispered hoarsely, "A GHOST BEHIND ME!"

And Grandma's full wrath was on Para now.

"Hey, Para, don't you have any other business? See, how you have scared the wits out of this child with your stupid stories. Any more of this and see what I would do to you!" she had said, glowering at Para, while rubbing the back of Ambe reassuringly.

But, for the children who rushed to their Grandma's house no sooner their school vacation started,—the main attraction was nothing but Parakka's stories— scarier, the better.

Parvati, or Para—Para*kka* to the children—was a very distant relative of the family and had come to stay with it when she was widowed, bringing along her only child, and had then become an integral part of the household. Cooking, tidying up, looking after nursing mothers or preparing pickles and *papads*,—she became indispensable in that house.

The story continued.

Bhīma commanded the respect and loyalty of the tenants of his land and also of people in the surrounding area, not to speak of the fact that they utterly feared him too. His shrewdness and sense of justice was well known even in the neighbouring towns and villages. His was the final word when it came to settling disputes.

Para's description of Bhīma's grand coach appeared to be never ending. Beginning with the magnificent horses, through the wheels, the holding stakes, the whip, the seats,—the grandeur of it all came out in great, graphic details. Listening to this, Ambe was carried away to that old time.

Para's stories seemed to get etched in the memory of the children who listened to them. So, even today, after many years, Ambe remembers the characters of Para's stories so vividly that she would often find resemblance of persons she saw on the road, train, bus or in a cinema to the fictional characters of Para's stories, as though they were her old acquaintances.

Parakka was now saying, "Bhīma's visit to the town meant that the coach had to be readied and he had to dress up. And in what great regal attire . . . The turban with brocaded edge and a silk shawl draped around the shoulders made him absolutely stand out! And when he rode in the coach like a lord, people crowding the street would drop the business on hand and stand staring at him, dumbfound in admiration. He was handsome as the Ravana himself.

"At least once a week he would go to the nearby town, which was just three miles away. Kashibai, his beloved mistress, lived there near the temple.

"Mind you, in those days a man was considered no good if he didn't have at least one mistress.' What a worm!' they'd sneer. And Bhīma was more than well endowed,—very rich and strikingly handsome to boot. He could afford four of them if he wanted to. But he was a man of principles,—just his wife at home and Kashibai on the side.

"When Bhīma showed affection for the tenants of his land, he really went overboard—he would build houses and buy clothes for them or fill their homes with all kinds of things. But if he disliked any,—that could be the end of that man. It is said that once he even had a tenant's hut razed, and got the place ploughed and sown to make it appear like a field,—all in the course of a night.

"Any opposition drove him mad. You know what? Some tenant had failed to pay him the rent for the land, and when argument followed, the tenant talked back— and that unleashed his explosive fury!

"Bhīma roared, 'Catch him and tie him to the pillar.' And the fellow was tied to this very pillar in this lower hall, and Bhīma himself took the whip and struck him relentlessly till the skin peeled off and blood oozed out."

Parakka's words caught it all,—the way Bhīma stood with the whip in his hand, how deftly he used it with a steely resolve in his eyes. Hearing this, and realizing that it had all happened in this very hall of this very house, the children got goose pimples.

When Parakka narrated Bhīma's misdeeds, it was with great pride and relish, as if she was singing paeans to a hero. It had been always so for her with anything connected with that house,—nothing but blind admiration and devotion—and it showed up in her every deed and word.

"Bhīma visited the town regularly every Friday. The merchant community had an upper hand in the town. They were all quite envious of Bhīma's style and haughty good looks. They bowed in front of him but sharpened their knives behind him. The merchants needed Bhīma for financial deals and settlement of disputes. So they submitted to him, and flattered him,—but muttered among themselves—We will deal with him and his coach when the time comes.

"And one Friday when Bhīma had gone to the town as usual, he saw 'Ranganna of the Cloth-Shop' in the company of his beloved Kashibai. It made him so mad with rage that he shot him dead on the spot with the gun that he always carried with him.

"And you know which gun was that? It is the same one which is now hung on the wall upstairs,—of course, now it is kept there for mere show. Imagine, Bhīma had taken that very gun . . . ."

"Parakka! Parakka! That gun is no longer there now. When I went upstairs to keep uncle's betel-box back in its place, the gun wasn't there! I swear,—I couldn't have missed it." Jagga interrupted excitedly.

"Shut up. You say it wasn't there? Where can it go? Did it grow limbs and walk away or what?" said Parakka, laughing it off and then continued with the story.

"The Friday next—Bhīma did go to the town for sure. But, when the tinselled coach returned home rider-less, what they found in it was his blood soaked body."

31

Parakka had presented the story so poignantly that brutish Bhīma's end brought tears to the eyes of the children. Ambe could not control her sobs.

"When Bhīma was leaving home that morning, the clerk, Subraya, had sought to stop him, saying—Not today, master! They say there is trouble in the town.

"But Bhīma,—would he ever listen? He got into the coach and rode off like a warrior going into battle.

"When he reached the town, it appeared quite normal on the surface. In the portico of Kashibai's house, everything was set for a session of cards. Rampa-Sowkar 'of the Grocery Shop', 'Coffee-Powder' Jannappayya and the rest of them were already seated. Bhīma, taking his usual place, said to himself,—That Subraya gets scared too easily. Why, the whole, dumb bunch is sitting here with their tails between their legs!

"The play was just about to start . . . ." As Parakka continued, repeated calls for her from Nani, the kitchen help, stopped the story in its tracks. Nani said some visitors were here and the master of the house had ordered coffee and snacks to be made ready for them in a jiffy,—whereupon Parakka sprang up from the floor and vanished into the kitchen. The story remained suspended.

Neither Ambe nor the other children had the slightest inkling that the half-told-story would never be concluded.

Para had extremely high respect for her master,— Ambe's uncle. Though she was older than him, she always referred to him as 'master' or 'our master'! His words were like commandments for her.

If the master of the house said, "It has been days since we had '*kadubu*", a flurry of activities would start in the kitchen instantly, ending with steaming hot '*kadubu*' being served the very next day by Para to her 'master'.

If, while eating '*pathrode*' made by her, he said, 'No pathrode can come anywhere near this' or 'Only Para can make such delicious *pathrode*'—it would make her so proud that her nose would be in the air for days on, whereupon the house-accountant Kittanna was likely to comment on the side, 'Except that it is so itchy to the throat,' and Para was sure to counter, 'You are too finicky Kittanna. If you carried less tales that throat of yours won't itch so badly.'

The children dispersed soon after Para left. Ambe and Meenakshi took up stringing the *Gorate* flowers, which they had plucked in the morning and had left in the corner of the middle room in a heap. When they finished, though a minor dispute arose as to whose string of flowers was longer, it mercifully ended with nothing more than the two of them making faces at each other. And then they helped each other in wearing those garlands, stringing them across their twin braids.

As Meenakshi started a game of '*chennemane*' with Vishwa,—Ambe, hopping and running, dashed through the rooms to the kitchen. The large kitchen was quite dark, though it was bright outside being only four o'clock in the afternoon. When she stepped into the kitchen with its soot covered walls, it took some time for her eyes to get adjusted to the darkness inside. Slowly, as the details were revealed, Parakka could be seen, busy preparing snacks.

The moment she smelt the sweet smell of '*sheera*', Ambe felt it must indeed be a very special guest who had come.

Parakka filled '*sheera*' and '*upkari*' tightly into two small cups and then kept them in the shelf above the hearth. No need to specially mention that it was meant for her darling son Lachanna, that is, Laxminarayana. If he was home, Ambe knew, he would be the first to be served by his mother with great fanfare. In any case, others could be served only after providing for him. Ambe was aware that her mother and her aunts often grumbled about this weakness of Para,—obsessive love for her son.

Ambe's grandma had this to say, 'She is quite all right,—but for this one fault. Anyway, let it be,—after all things get done. So, I turn a blind eye.'

There was an atmosphere of hustle and bustle both within and outside the kitchen. Nani and Kittanna were running between the kitchen and the outer hall carrying plates full of '*sheera*' and '*awalakki*', bananas heaped on trays, as well as tumblers, spoons and flasks. There was nobody to bother about Ambe.

Finding her mother chatting with her sisters on the swing-bench in the *chowki*, Ambe went to her, buried her face in her lap and whispered, 'Amma, I am feeling hungry.'

She was promptly rebuked by her mother, 'what is the hurry my girl,—let the guests finish!'

Ambe thought bitterly,—lost in their chatter, my mother and aunts do not know what is going on in the house! They could have made Para give the stuff to me to eat instead of keeping it aside for Lachanna. Ambe's feelings were strong.

The children had as much contempt for Lachanna as they had affection for Para. For whatever reasons and whenever they could, they tormented him—ridiculing him, making faces at him, hiding his things and so on. Parakka and Lachanna were two quite unrelated persons as far as they were concerned. Added to that, Lachanna looked quite different too,—short, squat and dark as against her lean and fair looks.

Para's fondness for her precious son knew no bounds. Though he was over twenty-five, he was still a child for her. When he ate, she sat by his side to encourage him to eat, ending up virtually feeding him. And what a celebration she made of his taking an 'oil-bath',—keeping hot water ready for his bath, massaging him with oil, rubbing his back as she poured water on him and so on! Also it was quite something when she called him by his full name, Laxminarayana,—crushing it fondly to '*Laxmarna*'.

Laxminarayana, or Lachanna, jobless after finishing his school, was wiling away his time wandering about. He would leave home in the morning only to return late in the evening. But when at home he would only do some minor chores like trimming the plantain leaves, stripping the coconut shell or cleaning the glass shades of the lanterns. Ambe had overheard her aunt saying in frustration, 'The boy is too lazy. It'd be ruination to depend on him!'

A subject of ridicule by everyone was Parakka's frequent exorcism of 'evil eye' that she thought befell her son regularly. If he just sneezed a couple of times, or his temperature rose a wee bit, or even if he just came home tired from the hot sun—she would promptly take a fistful of garlic skin and mustard, move it around him, throw the stuff into the hearth, look with great satisfaction when it spluttered on the hot charcoal, and finally take a pinch of that ash to smear it on his dark forehead for exorcising the 'evil eye'.

When Ambe saw Meenakshi and Vishwa push aside the *chennemane*-board and climb onto the windowsill to look out, she too joined them. In no time, with other children joining in, crowd density went up significantly around the two latticed windows on either side of the inner-hall's door. But it was not possible for the children to fully understand the situation in the outer hall from here. To begin with, the window was too small, and added to the great effort it took to peer through those round and square holes of the wooden screen, the visibility was limited. The only thing Ambe could make out was that two policemen were talking to her uncle even as they were emptying the plates filled with snacks that were being served up to them.

No sooner the police uniforms were spied than there was a commotion followed by bewilderment, and also a lot of pushing and pulling for a better view. When one was viewing, another got impatient. There was much elbowing, shirt-pulling and even lifting up of the smaller ones to give them a chance to view. But when their aunts yelled, the windows had to be vacated. Upon hearing the word 'police', it was now the turn of the elders to crowd around the windows. Ambe was surprised to see her Grandma and the horde of aunts now peering and whispering, as if it was only now that they became aware of what was going on outside.

After the children got their share of the eatables, they were startled to hear Grandma make a terse statement—'No evening play today; early meal and then to bed before the lights are lit.'

Play was already at stake,—but now the half-finished story too was in jeopardy. They ran looking for Parakka. When they found her, the scene at the kitchen and its outer veranda had changed completely.

Parakka was wailing loudly and was beating her chest and forehead in terrible grief. She even struck her forehead against a pillar a couple of times when others pulled her back and made her sit down and consoled her. She was struggling to free herself from them, crying,—'Leave me alone.' When the children saw to their horror blood streaming down her forehead, they bolted from the scene.

The 'ganji-meal' was over before dusk, just as Grandma had ordered, and the children were given a wash and tucked into bed early.

Dense dark night seeped into the room, which was anyway dark even during the day. Ambe's heart was pounding to an unknown fear.

Watching the flickering oil-lamp, it seemed to Ambe that the halo around it was enlarging and then diminishing, finally gobbling up the room in its surging waves. As fear churned her stomach, she pulled up the blanket to cover her face in an effort to fall asleep.

Even under the blanket cover, Ambe began to feel that Vishwa and Jagga, whose beds were near the door, were up to some mischief. When she pulled aside the blanket a bit to peer, she saw the two boys darting in and getting back to the beds,—and whispering among themselves.

"What Jagga, what's going on outside?" Ambe asked, unable to suppress her curiosity.

Ignoring her, the two went on whispering, and when she asked the question again, she felt her voice trembling.

"Timid girls should just lie in bed," was all that she got in reply.

Ambe crawled out of her bed, blanket wrapped around, and passing the beds of Meenakshi and Nimmi, sat on Jagga's bed, pleading, 'Tell me, please!"

"So, you can take it? Now listen,—Lachanna is dead and gone!" whispered Vishwa fiercely.

Ambe's eyes widened and she tried to wrap the blanket around her more tightly.

"They have laid him on the floor of outer veranda,—blood splattered all over the body. They say he fell from a tree." said Jagga.

Ambe started trembling perceptibly.

When,—after making sure no one was around,— the two boys were preparing to make one more foray outside, Ambe pleaded that she be allowed to go with them. "Okay, you can come. But not a syllable!" they decreed.

They stole through the inner hall and quietly entered the room beside the veranda where coconuts were normally stored. When she saw the pitch-darkness inside, Ambe felt she should not have come. But it was too late for that.

They climbed the pile of coconuts gingerly, a step at a time, to look through the tiny vent near the ceiling. Ambe hitched up her long skirt with one hand

and gripped the bars of the window with the other. And suddenly she slipped and tumbled down to the rumbling sound of the rolling coconuts. She was unaware if she screamed or cried. All she knew was that her mother, who just then appeared on the scene, pinched her cheek and thigh and then with profuse admonishments sent her back to her bed. Also, Ambe heard the thuds of the blows that fell on the backs of Jagga and Vishwa.

With the solemn warning that anyone who got up again will be skinned alive, Ambe's mother left the room, closing the door behind her.

As Ambe sobbed without let up under the cover of the blanket, she had to listen to the jeers of Jagga and Vishwa, who said things like, "But for this little demon . . . ."

Ambe eventually cried herself to sleep. And, when she got up in the morning, she had high fever and her eyes were burning, and she felt utterly weak. She had a strange feeling of floating in a pool of blood.

When Ambe's 'Little' Auntie came and saw her, she got alarmed and called Ambe's mother. And together they carried Ambe in her mattress to the outer room.

"Amma, am I going to die?" Ambe asked, crying.

"Don't say such things, dear. It's all for the good! It only means that you have become a grown-up girl today, my dear," consoled her mother.

But Ambe overheard her mother muttering to 'Little' Auntie, "Why did it have to happen here. It is her bad luck! Poor thing! She doesn't know a thing about all these customs here,—defilement, pollution, isolation and what not! How can she understand these things,—tell me, Siri."

39

Confined to that outer room for next three days, and as she lay in bed in fever and pain, Ambe could hear snatches of conversations as if in a long dream.

She heard her Grandma, "Say, I can't bear to see the misery of this Para. All that mollycoddling of the son! This is what came out of it."

Then somebody said, "That Lachanna was no ordinary person! He was very scheming, and Kittanna says that his mischiefs were too many!"

Someone else was commenting in a low voice, "You won't believe. He has been working on the tenants of the land and creating trouble for the master. It's good that someone got rid of him. He was a big nuisance anyway."

Ambe was delirious, uttering things like,—'Parakka', 'Lachanna', 'I am dying', and her body shook up every now and then.

Though the fever had subsided, she had not fully recovered when the voice of the farm hand, Mennka, came floating into the room, alerting her. Mennka, who was cutting grass for the cattle-feed, was talking in a low voice to Ganapu, who was cleaning the cattle shed.

"Ganapu, do you know,—I believe those paper pieces were found in the attic Monday morning. And when the master read it, they say he became furious and stormed out of the house with a gun in hand. For Lachanna,—the time for his end had come. This shouldn't have happened to a good man like him."

Ambe froze.

And then it all came to her. The children were playing hide and seek that morning. Ambe, who had scrambled up to the attic in a hurry to hide, had found a stack of those papers right by the side of Lachanna's box. The bright red pamphlets with pictures of hammer over sickle had caught the fancy of the children for a while, and seemed to be in every child's hand,—quickly turning into paper-boats and even small kites. But it was Ambe who had collected all the remaining papers and handed them over to her uncle dutifully.

"Amma!!" screamed Ambe,—loud enough to raise the roof.

Her mother came running, and wiping the sweat on Ambe's brow with a towel, asked her solicitously, "Why dear. What happened? You had a bad dream?"

"Amma, I want to go home . . . I Can't stay here anymore. Let us go right now, Amma," pleaded Ambe and kept on with it.

"Don't be adamant, dear. We shall leave tomorrow for sure. Don't you know that tomorrow is the fourth day? You will have a bath and then you will be out of this room for good. So, we will go home soon after that, okay?" her mother said, making up to her. But Ambe stuck to the refrain,—

"I don't want to be in this house any more . . . not at all . . . ."

THE SCENT OF JASMINE

When I saw Brigitte for the first time in our Manhattan office, I had instantly remembered Raji, but don't know why. Her facial features hardly resembled Raji's. Unlike Raji's long stick-like face, Brigitte had a wide face set with green luminous eyes. If Brigitte's complexion was lily-white with a tendency to turn crimson when she as much as raised her voice, Raji's was dusky.

But there was something of Raji in Brigitte. May be it was her broad square shoulders. Or, the way she quickly ran the brush through her hair and the speed with which she then put it away. It could be her let-me-take-control-of-the-situation way of making people get started at one go. Or, it could be the way she stood with her arms akimbo.

When I joined our office in Manhattan, Brigitte was away in the zonal office for some time. The day she came back, she had walked in briskly and directly to her place, switched on her computer, her shoulders set squarely, taken out a small brush from her purse and in just a couple of deft strokes combed her hair up in the front and down at the back, like men do, and got started on her work. Perhaps it was primarily the way she turned, her shoulders squarely angled, that brought Raji's memory back in a flash.

Later on when she was explaining to me the new accounts package, I got the opportunity to see her at close quarters and to know her better. As she did the explaining, craning her neck and manipulating the mouse rapidly, her sharp look was sheer Raji explaining some algebra problem to me back during my school days. Raji relished mathematics. When Raji explained and solved the problem in a jiffy and we did not digest it equally quickly, it would greatly annoy her, and meant real trouble for us.

One day, sitting in the cafeteria, I was telling Brigitte about Raji. Fixing me with her green eyes, she had said, 'Yeah, some people stay within us forever.'

It is about fifteen years or so since Raji died. She was a few years older than I was. I was then in my first year of college.

One couldn't call Raji with her long stick-like face pretty, but her face had a definite attraction. With the *pallu* of her sari folded and pinned tight over her chest, she looked ready for battle anytime. And that fold never moved even an inch across her flat chest and remained fixed right through the day.

When the college opened in our town, it was already two years since Raji had finished her matriculation. She had battled it out at home with a hunger strike and sundry acts of protest before she was allowed to join college. That, in a way, I think, made things easy for us when our turn came. Ours was a joint family and Raji, being the first daughter of the eldest uncle, was like an elder sister and a role model for all of us girls in the family. Like she was the first to join college, she was also the first to take up a job later on. That is a long story, anyway.

No sooner had she finished college, than Raji started applying for a job. It came as a surprise to the family, though her intentions of taking up a job could hardly have been unknown to anyone. For, through the three years of her degree course, she had frequently made reference to it. Like if grandma complained about her spectacles, Raji would say, 'Ajji, just wait till I finish my B.Com. The very next day after I take up a job you will get your new pair. Is that okay?'

Grandma was sure to retort, 'What job? It was a big mistake putting you in the college. You talk anymore about the job, I will tell your father to pull you out and marry you off. Got that?' Raji would just brush off grandma's threats and say, 'What is this nonsense about marriage? Forget it, Ajji!'

Everyone thought Raji wasn't serious when she made such disclaimers about marriage. So, none expected her to oppose the marriage proposal when the time came. But oppose she did, and ultimately in such a manner that even after so many years, the very thought of it chills me.

Raji had that reckless bravery, the kind which makes people take a plunge without a thought for the consequences.

Grandma used to say, 'that girl is more a tomboy . . . . nothing girlish about her . . . . No charm, no grace, and blunt to boot.'

Grandma, funny enough, could turn the very same argument upside down in praise of Raji, 'Whatever you may say . . . Raji is a great strength when she is around. She is a brave girl . . . unlike the rest of you. You feel safe in her hands!' Grandma said it all.

You had to be with Raji and experience that serene sense of safety to know what Grandma meant. Whenever we children got into any kind of trouble, it was Raji to whom we turned to. If I mentioned to her that someone in my class had broken my slate, she would say, 'Is that so? We will take care of it!' and during recess would head straight to my class. There were occasions when even our neighbours and acquaintances would take their grievances to her. Sometimes she would act on her own, when her mother was sure to shout, 'Now then,—whoever asked this girl go in there?' But Raji would not be bothered and went ahead anyway.

For Shyamali from our neighbourhood, Raji was a shield against the world. Once, I remember, Shyamali had come running to her complaining about a boy who had hit her with a rubber ball and in no time at all Raji had caught up with him, snatched the ball from him, tore it into two and threw the pieces in his face.

There were situations when I had told her about some problem of mine and had regretted it instantly. Like the time I told her about Bijju-teacher hitting me on my knuckles with a cane. It was a clear lapse on my part to have told this to Raji, for she marched straight away to the teacher, with me in tow. But when I remember her talking to Bijju-teacher with her hand on my shoulder, I can still feel the assurance of her touch.

As I came to know Brigitte better, I started liking her for her ways with the people, her interests and her keen observations on life. Her views about a new book or some new trend in art used to fascinate me. Through her I got introduced to the world of art, in a way. Because of her artist friend Judy, the three of us visited Metropolitan Museum of Arts for a special exhibition and at the time of Judy's solo art exhibition, I too did some running around with the two of them.

One afternoon in the office, Hilary, an accounts assistant in our department who sat next to me, called me and made signs with her eyes to look in the direction of Brigitte. Nick Taylor, the newly appointed graphic designer was trying to joke with Brigitte. 'Look at the courtship; the poor fellow doesn't probably know that Brigitte is already married!' Hilary winked. I did not understand and I looked at her questioningly.

'Brigitte and Judy are as good as married.' Said Hilary and whispered hoarsely and enthusiastically in my ear, 'She is a lesbian!' Obviously Hilary was not unaware of the effect of this information on me. I fell silent.

Though I already knew that Judy and Brigitte lived together, Hilary's revelation triggered some distressing echoes in my mind, which left me distracted for several days.

Later one morning in the office, when I had arrived at my table, I saw a note stuck to my pen stand and it said, 'Two tickets for Chicago beneath this,—for you and Mahesh. Don't miss it. Brigitte.' Nothing short of an order! But Brigitte's crisp message made me smile. Mahesh, my husband, and I had been planning for a long time to go to that musical.

All of us enjoyed the play, and after coming out of the theatre, when I wanted to pay Brigitte for the tickets, she refused to accept the money. Instead she playfully made a weepy face. 'I've been watching your face for days now. Tickets were the treatment for it,' she said with a pat on my back, while Judy asked me, 'So you are okay now?'

As the days passed, my feelings towards Brigitte slowly came out of the shadows of my mind. And just then one day, it so happened in the office that I slipped on a pencil lying on the floor and fell flat on my face, my forehead hitting a corner of a table in the process. I had almost passed out, and when I came to, I was lying on a table. A small bump had materialized on my forehead above my eye, and when I was getting up, Brigitte came in and said, 'Let us go to my apartment right away. You could rest for some time and then take the subway home.' She stood with her arms akimbo, as was her wont, when she spoke. I did not like the assertive tone,—or was it the way she stood. Something from the past troubled me. Then I did the stupidest thing. I had started sobbing suddenly and uncontrollably. This was utterly unlike me.

Our own emotions can give us a nasty surprise sometimes. Anyway, there I was sobbing and I felt awfully ashamed of myself.

Whenever I was sharply reminded of Raji, a range of emotions would rise within me—a sense of disapproval, a kind of sorrow, and a sudden rush of affection—all of which would torment me and exert great mental pressure. Perhaps this is what happened when Brigitte stood there and said, 'Let us get going,' in her usual authoritative tone.

At Brigitte's home, when her friend Judy saw the bump on my forehead, she brought an ice-cold poultice for it. Sharp featured and rosy cheeked, Judy had enviable waist that appeared narrow enough to fit in a fist. Her dress clung close to her skin. It was a delight watching her move about, light-footed as a ballerina, humming to herself. Brigitte came carrying a tray containing three cups of coffee foamed to the brim and some muffins. Sitting relaxed in an armchair sipping coffee, my mind slowly attained some balance.

As I watched the two of them in the golden glow of the late winter afternoon, hearing their soft chatter and the intimate domestic sounds, and seeing the closeness and ease of their relationship, I felt as if a part of my life which had been lost to me long ago has been rediscovered and as if a horrible knot in a remote corner of my mind was finally getting unravelled. As I settled into peace with myself, I felt like talking to them about Raji, about my grandmother and about Shyamali.

During my grandma's last days, when she was totally incapacitated, it was Raji who used to move her around for her bath and such things, although my mother used to feed her and look after her in general. Raji could carry grandma with such ease and set her down 'like a flower'—as grandma would put it—that grandma would not allow even Madhava, my strapping brother, to carry her. Raji was in the final year of graduation then. It was on the day of her final exam that Grandma died. Everyone at home, including her father suggested that Raji skip her exam, but she went ahead and appeared for it anyway. It was very much like her.

When Shyamali, our neighbourhood friend, fell seriously ill due to typhoid, she would have almost died but for Raji. It was Raji who got her admitted to the hospital and did the running around.

Shyamali had lost her parents in childhood and was staying with some relations of her for schooling and did some household chores for them in return. Slender as a reed, she was as fair and delicate as a wax doll. She was in Raji's class and used to accompany us while going to school. After returning from school in the evening, while most of us would go into our houses directly, Raji and Shyamali would usually linger at our gate and chat for a long time. Their long chats at the gate had become the talk of the neighbourhood. During holidays, it appeared as if there was no reprieve from their talking and laughing. Though I used to join them often and was accepted as well, a sudden and vague feeling of being an outsider crept up on me once in a while. At times I would imagine that either they suddenly stopped talking or changed the subject when I joined them.

Everyone called Shyamali 'Raji's tail' because the two appeared so inseparable. For Shyamali, Raji was always right in whatever she did or said. The two of them shared all the usual young girls' possessions—whether it was chocolates to munch or flowers to wear in the hair. Shyamali could not wait till she ran and gave her share to Raji and Raji was even more willing to reciprocate, invariably setting aside Shyamali's share with the words, 'Let the poor thing have it.' Gradually

Raji stopped the practice of even making such comments and we girls took it for granted that whatever Raji possessed, Shyamali had naturally a right to it. But there were occasions when this bothered me, even though I was quite fond of Shyamali.

In a way, everyone in our house was sympathetic to Shyamali. I had a special reason to like her because she was the one who came to my rescue in my craft-work like stitching or paper-folding. She was also the one who always rallied when I called her to play throw-ball, 'ring-game' or hopscotch. But, in spite of such a close alliance, if a quarrel ensued with her at school or playground and she threatened to take the issue to Raji, I never hesitated to fight for my right over Raji, saying, 'Look, Raji is my *akka*, not yours, mind you.' But looking back now, it is apparent to me that the bond between them was more than some family relationship or mere friendship.

'You said it, Geeta. You are absolutely right,' said Brigitte.

Meanwhile, Judy, standing in front of the mirror, appeared frustrated in her attempts at colouring her hair with thin streaks of some dye. 'Oh! It is just impossible.' she cried, stamping her foot.

'Give it to me, let me try,' said Brigitte taking the thin brush and the bottle of the dye from her.

'Geeta, do you know when I met this girl first? It was at my aunt's place—my mother's sister that is—and it was a Christmas party. We got interested in each other in no time at all . . . . pretty soon afterwards she moved in with me.'

'What about your parents?' I asked hesitatingly.

Her mother was more of a problem, she said. 'I had lots of difficulty in convincing my mom that there was no way I could spend a lifetime with a guy!' A slight shiver seemed to go through her as she lived the idea for a moment. 'She had the shock of her life when I told her so.' Brigitte said.

Then her voice softened, 'To tell you the truth, it was really my Mom who had sent me to the party at my aunt's that day. She and my aunt together had planned a husband for me—I was supposed to meet that guy and fall in love. Instead I met this one' at this Brigitte tapped Judy's head lightly with the back of the brush, 'and got stuck for good.'

Judy sat in front of Brigitte on a stool and, picking up a few strands of her hair, offered it to Brigitte for dying, warning her against any botch-up.

Judy's parents were apparently still cross with her, for she presently said, 'It is after all my life and I leave them to theirs.'

Shyamali had dense, black hair, reaching down to her hips. Raji loved to comb her hair. Whenever she dropped in at our house in the mornings with her hair undone, Raji would oil it and weave it into two long tapering braids.

After Shyamali finished high school, her education stopped and she remained at home doing the household work. Even when she was schooling, the pressure of the domestic chores was so much that she could hardly do her schoolwork and sometimes even had to skip school. During such times Raji pitched in for her, doing Shyamali's homework, writing notes for her or coaching her in maths,—all at the risk of neglecting her own studies. Such single-minded attention to Shyamali irritated me sometimes.

I remember one early morning when I was preparing for the dreaded maths exam and Raji sat there furiously scribbling notes for Shyamali with little concern for me. Suddenly, I stood up glowering at Raji and pressing my books against my chest, told her, 'you would not be bothered in the least if I failed in the maths exam, would you?'

Every word of mine must have been spat out with unbearable anger. But, it made Raji laugh uncontrollably. Closing her book, she came and hugged me and said, 'Okay madam; let me teach you some maths.'

Raji used to laughingly narrate this incident later on, whenever she could. Sometimes Shyamali too would be a part of this mirthful remembrance. At such times, I felt that Shyamali had no right to join in. And pulling a face, I made it clear that it was no laughing matter for me.

To this Brigitte said, laughing, 'I know!'

Judy, who was standing in front of the mirror fixing clips in her hair, stopped grooming herself and started giggling. She puffed up her cheeks to tease me. I could not help laughing, and I picked up a nearby flower vase and held it up threateningly. Feigning fear, but laughing all the same, Judy ran to Brigitte pretending to hide behind her. And holding Brigitte's shoulder she looked over it at me.

Brigitte said, 'Okay, okay.' Holding Judy's hand, which was over her shoulder, she looked at me as if to say, 'now what?'

Memories came flooding into my mind at that moment of a long forgotten evening at a temple. I do not know why I remember this particular incident so clearly when many of the details of the past have slipped off the edge of my memory. There was to be a special 'flower-*pooja*' offered by my grandma to the goddess at the Devi temple that evening. So, earlier in the afternoon, we girls and women of the house were sitting in front of a heap of flowers to string them into garlands.

Our whole house was filled with the sweet smell of jasmine flowers. Raji had the quickest hands among us in stringing the flowers and she also did the supervising of our work. Just as we finished making the garlands, grandma said wistfully, 'Now there, if everything goes well with Raji's marriage, I'll offer one more 'flower—*pooja*' to goddess Durga next year.' and joined her hands in prayer.

My aunt, Raji's mother, with a face that looked wracked with anxiety, said, 'What to say, this girl is growing up like a coconut tree and god knows where the boy for her is waiting.'

Aunt could hardly complete her sentence before grandma interjected, 'You can neither stop a good thing from happening nor a bad thing from not happening. Why are you worrying so much anyway? Listen to me. I have worked out everything. You know the boy Prema mentioned when she came the other day—the boy from Koteshwara, I mean. He is the one. I've already given Raji's horoscope, and if the horoscopes match, there is not going to be any delay . . . . It'll be as soon as the exams are over . . . no looking here and there.'

Grandma was as assertive as ever. 'But Athe, she has to agree after all.' Aunt said, working herself to exasperation.

'She jolly well has to!' grandma declared with supreme assurance.

Raji acted as if she did not hear a thing. Shyamali sat nearby with head bent down.

It was only when I heard Raji's rather gravelly voice, 'Hey, what is the matter with you, Shyamali?' that I looked up and saw that Shyamali's face had suddenly puckered up as if she was going to cry. Seeming to suppress the sobs by biting her lip, staring at the string in her hand, she neither looked up nor said a word.

My words, 'Why Raji, what happened?' did not appear to register with them at all. And Raji, resting her hand reassuringly on Shyamali's shoulder, and looking at her lowered face, whispered, 'don't be afraid, Shyamali. Let them talk as much as they like. But it is I who has to marry, right? And grandma has no other business after all!'

Bending to look at Shyamali's face, she said again, 'After I go to Mangalore and set up a house, you can come and stay with me. If you like, you can even go to college, what do you say?' Raji could as well have been cajoling a child.

Shyamali now looked up and smiled weakly with tearful eyes. The way they looked at each other said something, I thought. At that very moment I suddenly realized that there was a secret between them, which I would not be able to understand.

After the garlands were placed in the boot of our car and the car was filled with people to its capacity, it was decided that Raji and Shyamali would walk to the temple.

Yelling, 'I too will walk!' I ran to them and walked with them to the temple which was only a short distance from our home.

Inside the temple, oil-lamps flickered in the semi-darkness. Jasmine garlands were festooned all over the place. The air was thick with the intoxicating fragrance of jasmine and the temple was filled with worshippers. Raji and Shyamali stood holding hands in the faint glow of the lamps till the *arti* was over. I had not left their side for a moment.

I saw Shyamali whispering into Raji's ears and I caught Raji's words, 'Yes, like you swear upon water . . . . or fire . . . . here it is . . . . Flowers . . . .'

The temple bells were ringing non-stop and the voices were not distinct. My question—What? Swearing upon flowers?'—was completely drowned in the continuous din.

After receiving the *prasad* from the priest, when we were coming out of the temple, I saw Raji fixing the flowers in Shyamali's hair.

Brigitte who has been listening intently, exclaimed, 'How beautiful!' She was still holding the hands of Judy, which were on her shoulders, and Judy, who rested her chin on Brigitte's head, was looking at me brightly.

'Even as you were describing it, the scent of jasmine filled my nostrils.' said Judy, taking a deep breath, with eyes half closed, like she was savouring the fragrance. She went on, 'this is love—like the spreading of fragrance, like the running of a stream, like the singing of a song . . . .'

Strangely, I had stopped talking to Raji sometime before her death. It was out of some childish spite. It was not like I had completely severed ties with her, but more like I was not talking to her directly. It was actually a subtle way of ignoring her. Also, I started annoying her by doing some or the other uncalled for things—going off when she called me, pretending I did not hear her, doing exactly the opposite of what she wanted me to do and so on. It used to go to such a ridiculous extent that, for instance, when she reminded me of my homework I would say, 'Oh yeah? I just won't do it,' curling my lips for added effect. And I would really not do the homework and even get punished for it in the school. I do not know why I behaved as I did. After these many years it does seem strangely funny when I think of it.

The day Raji was setting off for Mangalore, I was cold with her, as was usual those days, and stood with my eyes averted. I was not as sorry that she was leaving us as I was angry that she looked so happy while packing up. Shyamali was going with her to help her with the setting up of the new house. This hurt me even more.

While they were standing near the car ready to go, I noticed from the corner of my eyes that they said something and then laughed looking in my direction. I also heard my mother saying, 'Oh! Geetu! She and her moods!' Raji called me to her, but I would not budge. She came to me and drawing me to her said, 'You still angry? Come to my house as soon as your vacation starts, okay?' and stroked my face. I felt like crying. Shyamali also came running to me and holding my hands, said, 'Geeta, good bye.' I wonder how I managed to maintain my disdainful look under the circumstances.

Leaning on the door-frame, my eyes still averted, whatever I had managed to see from the corner of my eye was the last impression of them I still carry with me—sitting by the car window and waving at us through the half lowered glass, calling us one by one to say goodbye, flashes of their smile and wind in their hair. I stood there appearing intent on unravelling a loose thread from my dress with a—what-if-they-go-I-couldn't-care-less attitude, and had not even bothered to wave to them.

Whoever thought that the two of them who left that day would never ever return? Within a short time of Raji going to Mangalore, her marriage proposal was finalized. Even as she continued to oppose the idea of marriage, my uncle—that is her father—had arranged for a meeting with the prospective groom and his family at his friend's place in Mangalore. Everyone agreed to the alliance and the date for the wedding was fixed. Marriage-in-May, just-two-months-away was how it was, when she died.

As I continued to narrate the story, I felt a lump in my throat. Brigitte, while removing the dry poultice from my forehead, said, 'Human nature is so complex—a lifetime is not enough to understand even a person who is very close to us . . . Right?' I could not agree more. Not just me, but all of us had failed to understand Raji. But I did not respond to Brigitte's rhetorical question. My throat was too tired and parched.

Though I sat there talking to them for a long time, I could not bring myself to say much about the manner in which Raji and Shyamali had died. But how much did I know about it anyway? Those days, there was a veil of secrecy about all matters touching even remotely on the prestige and honour of the family. By the time I came to know about it sketchily, I had got married and left the town.

I only knew that Raji had gone on a picnic one day to the beach at Ullal with her friends from the bank where she worked and had taken Shyamali along too. It was during that picnic, they said, that the two of them had drowned in the sea.

It was March and my school final exams were going on. The elders had left for Mangalore immediately. So, there were only children in the house, except for my mother, and she was in a strange, angry mood. I clearly remember that anything we asked drew some invariably absurd reply from her. A simple request for a pencil for the forthcoming exam would get a response from her like, 'No pencil, nothing! What great expectation can we have from this education? Nothing! This stub of a pencil is good enough for your stupid exam.' Or else, like, 'To hell with the pencil! Too much liberty has gone to your heads!'

Subsequently, there was such a rapid succession of events that there was little inclination or time to talk about this matter. And we children were too scared to talk about it anyway, as it appeared to be a forbidden subject. My Uncle died of a heart attack, Aunt lost her mind and was in the Kankanady hospital for months on end, the marriage of Padubidri-Aunt's daughter was cancelled—and as these tragic events played out one after another, taking us in their swirling currents, we, the children, had attained the status of 'grown-ups'.

It was several years after my marriage that I came to know that actually only two of them had gone to the beach that day. It was Madhava who told me about it. I had gone to visit him in Madikeri for a couple of days.

'Actually there was no picnic at all, Geeta! Only two of them had gone to the Ullal beach and there was nobody from Raji's office with them,' he told me. Also it was then that he had narrated to me his agonizing experience of emptying out Raji's rented house in Mangalore.

I remember how within a month of Raji's demise, Madhava had gone alone to Mangalore and brought back her things. I would never ever be able to forget that ashen face of his on that day. He did not speak a single word then. He had gone quickly up the staircase to the attic with Raji's trunk in his hand and her rolled—up mattress under his arm, and I had followed him. After putting down the things on the floor of the attic, he had sat hunched on the rolled mattress with vacant eyes. I had not dared to speak to him that day.

Regarding the letter left behind by Raji, I came to know of it from Aunt Nirmala during my recent visit to India.

When Nirmala narrated what was written in the note—'We do not wish to live apart. So we have decided to die together. Please forgive us'—it was as if the note was in front of me, with Raji's neat, left leaning long hand, with not a smudge or blotch on the sheet. I did not even miss her familiar signature with the last letter ending with a flourish and then curving around to underline it. 'What to say, it was destined.' Nirmala had sighed.

'I had gone there once before, you know,' said Nirmala. 'I had some work in Mangalore—now what was that . . . . ?' Nirmala was groping for the reason.

Knowing her fully well, I did not find it difficult to guess that it was plain curiosity which had taken her there. 'Yes! Now I remember,' she said, 'we had gone to Mangalore to buy saris for the festival and we said, well, Raji has set up her house here. Why not see it? And that is how we went there. 'He' was also with me.'

To this, my uncle who sat in the easy-chair with his hands cupped behind his neck, nodded silently. Uncle is a man of few words and with the recently developed pain in his knees, he speaks even less.

Nirmala said that she was astonished by the way the two young women ran the household—their irrepressible enthusiasm, their joint cooking, and their exceptional housekeeping. They kept saying, 'Look here *Mavayya*, see that *Athe*,' and showed them every nook and corner of the house.

'I say, we, who have managed our houses for so many years, are nothing compared to them.' Nirmala had declared then.

'When Raji went to the bank Shyamali would do the cooking, I believe . . . . Like two horses with one harness!' Nirmala added. Though said appreciatively, I could discern a trace of disapproval in it.

Nirmala had said that she was amazed by the rows of gleaming, stainless steel containers on the kitchen shelf—'all bought with the money she earned!' In the very next breath, lowering her voice, she had sighed, 'Poor thing! It hurts to think of it now.'

'Remember what my mother used to say about her? Raji could make the dead sit up . . . . Imagine that very

Raji took her own life!' Nirmala's tone had a tint of misgiving about Grandma's praise in retrospect.

Uncle, who was largely silent, started saying, 'Poor girls! Shouldn't have ended like this! Who knows . . . . ? What might have happened . . . . What feelings . . . . !' Uncle not only spoke less, but also spoke in a deliberate, staccato manner. Before he could complete his observation, Nirmala had interrupted him. 'No marriage . . . nothing! Leave us alone!—What does that mean?' she said as if challenging her husband.

Uncle freed his hand from the back of his head and placed it on the arms rest of the chair and said, 'If you ask me, Geeta, I would say your father and Uncle were in an unholy hurry.'

Nirmala would not leave it at that. 'Shyamali was too much. What kind of attachment was it anyway—unheard of! My brother sure made a rumpus about it—engagement has taken place so I'll see to it that the marriage will follow . . . It is a question of honour—! Of course, he went overboard in admonishing her, I agree. But he was right in what he said, wasn't he? You tell me.' She looked at me.

Taking off from where he had left, as if there had been no interruption from Nirmala, Uncle said resignedly, 'Tell me, what is the use of raking up things now? It is . . . . tch . . . . Altogether . . . .' Holding to his knees, he got up and walked away, dragging his feet.

'All said and done, there is a notion that with marriage some how things will fall in place. Sometimes it doesn't turn out so.' Uncle said. He shuffled along, leaning sideways, and stepping out to the verandah, said almost to himself, 'They could have been left to themselves . . . . But the time was such . . . .' His words coming in through the door, braving the onslaught of Nirmala's voice, touched me.

I remembered then that Madhava had said something like it when I was in his house in Madikeri. It was a night during the initial days of monsoon. We were in the porch and it was raining outside incessantly. With a shawl draped around my shoulder, I was sitting cross-legged on the sofa. Madhava's wife sat on the floor leaning against the sofa. Madhava, sitting on the balustrade of the porch with his hands planted on it on either side, was talking.

The topic had somehow turned to Raji. Madhava remembered that it was on a similar rainy evening that he had gone to Raji's house to collect her things. The bank officials had waited for two or three months before they wrote to her father asking him to get the house vacated. Uncle had in turn telephoned Madhava, who was studying in Mangalore then, and told him to collect whatever he thought fit to collect and dispose the rest.

'The house was desolate . . . . Not a soul . . . My experience of entering that empty house was so devastating I wouldn't wish it for my enemy!' Madhava shuddered.

'And the same house—two months before they departed—was an utterly different scene and such a lot of fun.' he reminisced. He had then gone there to deliver a parcel from Raji's mother.

The two had pressed Madhava to stay for dinner and had joked that for someone eating junk at the hostel, it didn't make any difference where he ate. And then there had been great hustle and bustle in the kitchen with the promise of special dishes for him. It had reminded him of the 'house-house' we girls used to play not too long ago.

They had joked and laughed and in the process he ate till he was stuffed full. They chatted for a long time after dinner—about this and that, about Shyamali's joining college and so on.

"Talking and laughing, the time just flew.' he said. The embroidered covers on the back of the chairs, the knitted cloth on the table, the bead-work elephant hanging on the wall—Madhava described the house graphically to me. ' . . . All Shyamali's handiwork.' Raji had said, pointing at them in a complaining tone, but with scarcely concealed pride.

Madhava said that till he returned to that house later, he could not conceive how much a house could change in just about three months' time. As he described those moments, I could feel what he had felt on re-entering that house.

There was a steady drizzle in the gathering darkness of the dusk. When the door was opened and the light was switched on, the house was overwhelmingly silent. A few steps into the house—footprints on the thick layer of dust on the floor, shards of the broken glass pane, a pool of water in the corner that had seeped in through the window, the soggy and mouldy embroidered back-covers of the chairs, windblown papers stuck to the wet floor, the letters tossed in by the postman—now covered with dust. And he saw in the kitchen—cockroaches skittering around as if they owned the place, cobwebs between the shelves and the wall—and the wall and the roof, remnants of a sparrow's nest and dried up bird-droppings on the kitchen platform . . . .

Madhava, who stood in that two-room house, suddenly felt he was all alone in the whole world. And as this strange loneliness engulfed him, he was weighed down by unbearable melancholy.

But when he looked at the smile on the faces of Raji and Shyamali in their framed photograph on the wall, it seemed to Madhava that the two were not yet aware of the barren reality after their fragile dream had come to an end.

THE HOUSE THAT SOPHIE BUILT

They were going up the spiral staircase and Dora asked, "Is it the only way?"

"No dear, I think some sort of repairs is going on at the front . . . the way they have covered the front with jute cloths and corrugated iron sheets." said Vincent with a hint of an irritation. This is not the way he wanted Dora to see the Carvallho Villa.

"Actually this is a fire escape. Most of the old houses here have them at the back and, Dora, when we were children, we just loved this staircase, scrambling up and down all the time, using it as a hiding place and all,—it was great fun."

Vincent, turning around suddenly, bent down to make a mock attempt to grab Dora, saying, "How come we never kissed on a spiral stairway till now!"

Dora, who, ever alert to Vincent's quirky ways of romancing, had hopped down two steps smartly to dodge him, retorted—"because stairways are not for romancing."

"Careful, eh . . . Dora! Don't trust this rickety thing,—not meant for hopping and jumping, you know." warned Vincent, now going up again.

A little while ago, when they had alighted from the bus near Demonte Park, Dora had exclaimed, looking up and down Turner Road, "What a lovely place. It looks just like Mangalore!" The trees lining it on either side made a leafy arch over the road, and the evening sun's rays filtering through it suffused the whole area in an enchanting soft light.

"Just wait till I take you around, you would wonder if it is Kalyanpura, Udupi or what!" said Vincent like a proud explorer showing a newly discovered land.

Though it was more than two years since Vincent set up home in Borivili after getting married, he could not find time till now to take Dora to meet his Aunt Sophie. With both of them working, it was hard to find any time for outings in Bombay. But this Sunday Vincent was quite determined. They went to a restaurant for an early lunch and immediately thereafter set out for Bandra in a double-decker.

Throughout their journey from Borivili to Bandra, Vincent talked almost incessantly about his Aunt Sophie, her Carvallho family and the Carvallho Villa. The depth of his attachment surprised Dora.

Almost a hundred years ago, Aunt Sophie's father-in-law, the elder Carvallho, had 'run away' from his home in Mangalore due to some family dispute,—the details of which have been totally obscured by time. He had left his wife and children at home and lived alone as a tenant with one D'Mello family in Bandra for a rent of one and half rupee per month. It was this D'Mello who initially persuaded, and later on pushed the elder Carvallho to buy some land, when plots were up for lease in the adjoining area of East Indian Salsette Society at the rate of three rupees and eight annas per square yard. After buying the land, the elder Carvallho put up a two-room shack in the newly acquired piece of land and continued to live alone.

The Carvallho history rested there for a decade or so till his son Gregory came to Bombay looking for his father and found him.

Gregory took up a job as an assistant to a shipping agent and later set up his own shipping agency and still later, just before the second world war, made it big,—when many were jobless and desperate. When Gregory, on one of his visits to Mangalore, married Sophie and brought her to Bombay, the Carvallho history really took off.

Gregory loved his wife deeply and her every wish was an opportunity for him to show it. Sophie wanted to build a house where the shack they lived in stood. Elder Carvallho, who had come to like his young daughter-in-law, consented and Gregory gave her the free hand and money to build it. It was also the time, after two daughters, Sophie was carrying again.

Vincent had heard the story of how Sophie built the house from many among his relatives and on many occasions. The stories were so vivid that he almost felt that he saw it being built, though he was far from being born even.

He had heard, how she was on her feet all day,—supervising the construction, selecting the material, instructing the mason and carpenters and going into the minutest details. It was a passion for her. Vincent's uncle in Vakola used to say that, 'Sophie had struggled with each brick which has gone into building her house.' Vincent remembered his mother, a great admirer of her sister-in-law, saying, 'these marble and granite houses you see now-a-days . . . they are nothing compared to Sophie's house. Sophie has an eye for beauty, I tell you.' Aunt Clara would always admire, 'the red mortar floor of Sophie's house shines so well that you could do without a mirror.'

Within a year or so, in place of the two room shack stood a beautiful new house, the 'Carvallho Villa'

Vincent's Vakola-uncle had figured out that Sophie's passion for her house could be traced to her childhood in Kalyanpura, near Mangalore, when she and her widowed mother were practically rootless,—shifting from one relative's house to another, sometimes living virtually as maids.

There were a few in the family, who said that Sophie's attachment to her house was excessive,—especially since her visits to Mangalore and Kalyanpura became rare and then stopped altogether. 'She doesn't need anybody, now that she has her house,' was the usual comment made those days.

But it was patently wrong to say that Sophie forgot her relatives or her hometown. Not only had she named the house after the family, but welcomed both her and her husband's relations from Mangalore and Kalyanpura to come and stay with her for holidays. That is how Vincent, with his mother and many other relatives had spent quite a few Christmas holidays in 'Carvallho Villa'. In those holidays, the Carvallho Villa used to crawl with so many hyper active children that someone called it a Mini-Mount-Mary-Fair. It was Aunt Sophie who benignly managed this rampaging horde and called it to order for prayer and dinner.

There were of course bigger and more magnificent houses in the neighbourhood,—but none so beautiful and so to say, articulate. Heads turned involuntary towards the Carvallho house while people walked past it, 'just as it happens today,' added Vincent.

The front of the Carvallho Villa was a graceful semicircle with a colonnaded veranda running all around it. The front door opened to a corresponding semi-circular hall, the rear end of which was used as a dining area, and beyond that were kitchen, bath rooms and so on. The two staircases—one from the front and the other from the back—lead to the upper floor with balconies all around.

The façade of the house was unique because of exquisite wooden lattices which arched between the columns of the veranda and a luminescent panel of stained glass with pictures of angels and art-nouveau designs above the entry. The pale yellow wooden lattices forever looked fresh because Sophie had them coated every year with some specially formulated lacquer. A flag stoned driveway and an elegant iron gate completed the picture-like Carvallho villa.

Sophie planted trees all around the house,— coconut, jackfruit, *neem*, mango, *chikkoo*, Palmyra and many others, which would remind her of her beloved

Kalyanpura. They spread their foliage in many hued greens, creating an inviting cool shade. And then the birds came flocking in to inhabit the trees,—parrots, coppersmiths, orioles and the like.

Carvallho Villa, in a way, reflected Sophie's character,—quiet dignity, charm, openness and cohesiveness. It was a brief halfway house for many relatives and friends who came to Bombay in search of jobs or newly-weds and others on the lookout for a rented house or who came looking for family members who had left no trace after they left for Bombay from their hometowns near Mangalore. Sophie not only gave them shelter, but through her husband and friends of the family, helped them in getting jobs or obtaining rented accommodations or tracing their relations. Vakola uncle,—given to literary flourishes in conversation, had said that, 'Carvallho house has been an oasis to many a caravan. It became what the world could not be for the young Sophie and her widowed mother.'

The Carvallhos were a close-knit family bound together by shared values—love of God and such things. And Philip became an icon of all that,—Philip, whom Sophie was carrying when the Carvallho house was being built. He was born within a few months of the house warming. The baby boy and the new house were the twin joys of Sophie's life at that time.

Philip grew to be a handsome young man, and as many said, rarely did so many good qualities reside in one person as they did in Philip. Well behaved, ever helpful to neighbours and friends and greatly talented. Till today whenever the talk turned to Carvallho household,—the subject of Philip came up invariably.

And everyone had something good to say about him and the voices became softer, and a strain of longing for a precious thing lost was discernible.

After her husband died, Sophie became less sure of herself,—but Philip became her strength. But this did not last for long and the loss of Philip was the most severe blow to Sophie ever,—more severe blow than the death of her husband's was.

'Let alone Sophie, it has been a most severe shock to us, and remains so whenever we remember it, even today.' said people who knew the Carvallhos. There seemed to be a catch in Vincent's voice when he mentioned this. He himself had very fond memories of Philip.

'No one could remain the same after meeting Philip and none could remain the same after losing him either,' as Vakola uncle rightly said.

Sophie's second son Tony was different. '. . . Very different.'—Vakola uncle would have added. Tony was always in an unholy hurry and in a playful mood,—innocent, but naughty.

Now, as Vincent and Dora approached the landing on the first floor, they heard a sharp voice from above, "Look here child, see who is coming,—is it Philip?"

"It is Aunt Sophie. . . . . The voice is still the same." said Vincent to Dora.

"But Philip?" Dora's voice trailed off inquisitively.

Vincent whispered, "That is her elder son. He is no more, as I told you."

A young boy, about seven or eight years old, who had opened the door, yelled into the room, "Granny, someone is here."

"Who?" enquired the old lady, sitting on the sofa with her legs stretched.

"It is me,—Vincent,—Philomena's son. And this is Dora. Mother had been asking me to visit you." said Vincent. The boy repeated the very words at high volume.

"Oh! Vincent, eh? Which Vincent? Philomena's son . . . . ? Tell me so." Covering her toothless mouth with her palm, she said with quick laughter, "Come, come. Sit down. Philomena has no other business or what, asking you to see me with my one foot in the grave!" She now laughed heartily with her toothless mouth wide open.

'Aunt Sophie is a stickler for tidiness.' Vincent had said,—but Dora saw a messy room, with every nook and corner of it crammed with things, leaving no room to sit.

Vincent made some room for himself and Dora to sit on a divan, after pushing aside a tape recorder, a flower vase and few other things of their ilk.

"Look here . . . curse me . . . can't remember the name . . . .for the life of me. *Arrey*, you there, get some coffee and biscuits for the guests." The old lady called out to her daughter-in-law. A stern order was later issued to the boy to fetch his mother immediately.

The boy went in and came out with his mother.

"Work is going on . . . . That is why all this mess." Said the daughter-in-law apologetically, glancing side long at the old lady.

Aunt Sophie called the boy, "Hey, Philip, get me a sheet of paper . . . These mosquitoes are just driving me mad." And taking the sheet of paper from the boy, she started fanning herself vigorously with it.

The daughter-in-law smiled and said, "She calls people by which ever name that comes to her mind . . . . Even if there are no mosquitoes, she constantly complains about them."

The way Aunt Sophie was referred to, it was as if she was not physically present there,—the way the world adopts when the person referred to no longer counts.

The daughter-in-law made the inevitable enquiry, "How does Dora find Bombay?"

"Oh, she is getting used to . . . Though she gets scared sometimes by the crowds." said Vincent, looking at Dora smilingly.

"Get the guests some coffee! Chatting and wasting time! You should know better." said Aunt Sophie to her daughter-in-law.

"Sophie aunty, forget it! We are not guests really." Said Vincent raising his voice, by now realizing that talking low would not get him an audience here, "We already had coffee at home before we left." He added, and carried on with the raised voice, "Where is Tony?"

Before his voice had died down, Tony made a dramatic entry, pushing aside the door.

"*Ho! Ho*! Look here,—who but our Vincent Sahib! Long-time no see. Where have you been man?" Cried Tony at the highest possible decibels, and with a typical Bandra accent, "I was right there in the front yard man. Don't have a minute to spare and don't you ask me why!" Tony flailed his arms and shook his head,—all at once, creating the illusion of a minor storm.

"Look at him." Said Aunt Sophie disparagingly, "Always doing a jig. And how can he spare any time?"

"Mom! You have no idea at all. All that you know is how to run me down . . . . By the way Vincent, isn't it the first time you are bringing your wife here? How . . . . how does she find Bombay?"

Dora saw the truth of what Aunt Sophie said about Tony. Tony could never stand still as he spoke;—two steps backwards and two steps forward, and then he would step sideways. When he addressed Dora, he almost fell on her, tripping on the edge of a steel box lying around.

"Tony, I brought Dora here to show her the Carvallho house. Looks like some big repair work is going on." said Vincent.

Before he could finish the sentence, Tony sprang up to face Vincent, with his back to his mother and whispered hoarsely, "Man-O-man! *Shhh* . . . .! She is very clever, can even read lips."

Tony came very close to them and bending down, said in a conspiratorial low voice, "The old house is going down and a new building is coming up here. She doesn't know it,—but if she comes to know . . . ."—He stuck out his tongue and rolled up his eyes, "Vincent,—you know how sticky she is!" he said.

Vincent was shocked by this revelation. The rumour has been around for some time, but he had not believed it. It was unimaginable that Aunt Sophie,—who built this house lovingly, who loved this house so dearly and who lived in this house so grandly,—did not know that her house is falling?

Tony bent still more and laying his hand on Vincent's shoulder, said, "Come down,—I will tell you all!" and then straightening up suddenly and turning towards the door he said loudly, "Mom! I am going down."

"Hey, Tony,—where are you going? There are guests here. Have you spoken to them?" cried his mother.

Tony, with one foot already beyond the door, turned around to say, "Don't you know it is Vincent, Mom? Papa's sister's son! Or—your dear sister-in-law, Philomena's son!" He said in a voice loud enough to be heard in the street below before getting out of sight.

"What a fool I am!" said Aunt Sophie, striking her forehead with her palm and laughing, "Tell me so! If you talk in hush-hush tones,—how would I ever know? Come here son, and sit beside me. How is dear Philomena now?"

She took Vincent's hand in her own, when he came and sat next to her on the sofa.

"She is all right . . . And remembers you a lot." said Vincent.

"What did you say . . . Where has she gone?"

"No,—she didn't go anywhere. She is at home only. She remembers you a lot, I said."

Vincent felt self-conscious as he spoke at the top of his voice. He felt that it was as well if he had not spoken. It did not matter, he thought.

It could have been due to all that speaking aloud he did, or the situation in that crowded room, or the stunning news that Tony had just delivered,—Vincent's throat became hoarse.

As he looked at the wrinkled and stick-like hand that held his,—he suddenly felt that it was not the Aunt Sophie he wanted Dora to meet. In place of the stately and lively Aunt Sophie, whom he had seen lording over the Carvallho house, he saw a withering, senile woman.

"It is Jesus' Grace after all . . . . She got a good alliance . . . . And . . . The *jari* sari . . . ." Aunt Sophie was lost in the labyrinths of her memory. Vincent realized that for all the shouting he did, nothing of what he said reached Aunt Sophie.

Mother wanted to come to Bombay . . . Perhaps she would make it. She remembers you a lot and talks about you. But she has pain in the joints. She is weak and finds it hard to leave father alone . . .—Vincent wanted to say all these and more to Aunt Sophie. But could he shout out all these things,—and even then, could he be sure of Aunt Sophie grasping what he said? It looked so futile; Vincent quietly gave up the idea of any further conversation with his aunt.

Tony's wife returned with coffee and a plate full of biscuits. Vincent recognized instantly that the biscuits were from the Hersh Bakery on the road that ran behind the house. There used to be a line at the bakery early in the mornings for the bread. He remembered how he used to tag along, when Philip was sent by Aunt Sophie to fetch fresh bread from Hersh Bakery. It all came back to him in his mind,—the warmth of the fresh bread, the heady, appetizing smell that hung thick in the bakery, and the 'hellos' and 'howdy' among the neighbours who stood around in the early morning light.

"You will like it. The bakery here is famous."— Vincent heard Tony's wife saying to Dora.

Aunt Sophie, beady eyed rambled on, "Philomena's hair is always unruly,—and two braids . . . I used to . . . ." For her, past and present had become one seamless continuum.

"She forgets what happened a minute ago,—but she sometimes remembers every small detail of the past." said Tony's wife in a complaining tone.

Vincent drank his coffee hurriedly, intending to leave the place before Aunt Sophie would again ask who the guests were. Putting down the empty cups, Vincent said, "Sophie aunty, see you." and got up. As he and Dora hurried out of the room, they heard the voice behind them,—"Can't see a thing. . . . . And in addition these troublesome mosquitoes . . . . *Arrey* . . . . Looks like some guests have come."

Vincent and Dora walked around the house to the front, threading their way through heaps of rubble, stacks of steel rods and piles of cement bags and bricks. Tony, with his potbelly stuck out, was speaking to the workers. His words went helter-skelter in the din of the concrete mixing machine. Upon seeing Vincent, he rushed to him.

"You know what? Today we are going to cast the first slab! You have to pour concrete nonstop, man!" He said.

Vincent said weakly, "So the work has started already?"

"And what do you think! Before the front part of the house is brought down, I wanted everything to be shifted to the rear of the first floor, and then made it a practice to use the staircase at the back. And today we are ready to cast the first slab. The builder,—that Thadani fellow,—is really superb, man. . . . Number one builder,—no doubt about it. . . . Everything on time!"—while saying so, Tony called a couple of workers who were passing by and told them sternly,

"*Arrey, Dekho,* keep these things aside, or else someone might trip over them."

"I am surprised how Sophie aunty agreed to this." Vincent said, still in a state of shock.

Tony cleared his throat and laughed heartily.

"Never agreed . . . Listen to this. She doesn't know a thing,"—clapping his hands in a delight, Tony explained, "Got her signature saying that it was for a new water connection! Vincent, do you think it was possible otherwise? She is lost in the past. She kept saying 'no' all these years,—while all the owners of bungalows in the neighbourhood sold theirs and made their pile! Just look around,—Grace Villa on the right, Sony Cottage next to that, Simon Abode in front of the church,—all the bungalows have gone and buildings have come up. And she!—'not my Carvallho Villa' . . . . 'It will remain as it is!'—'My Bandra is being spoilt'— what nonsense! 'Her' Bandra! What does she think of herself? She's the queen of Bandra or what?" Tony had a good laugh.

"It is only in the last one year, after she had gone soft in her head that I was able to do something, man! Vincent, you tell me,—have I done anything wrong? You are smart,—just tell me . . . am I right or wrong? Is it a joke to maintain a bungalow these days?"

Poor Aunt Sophie has lost her mind and that has emboldened this rascal,—thought Vincent. If she had been in her proper mind, there was no way she would allow it. She would have rather thrown out her son,—if it came to that.

"She can't hear,—she can't see and she can't think. What difference any house would make for her. Tell me. Am I right or wrong?"

As Vincent watched the concrete being poured into the shuttering of the first slab,—a pair of eyes behind a window in the rear of the house caught his attention.

"Who is that?" asked Vincent.

"Where? . . . Where?" said Tony, hopping over a bent steel rod and looking up.

"Oh that! Jessie, she didn't meet you? It is four days since she had come."

Jessie was Tony's youngest sister.

By then Tony had shifted his position to the rear of the concrete mixing machine and was making signs to Vincent to come to that place. He perhaps wanted to avoid those eyes.

"Vincent, you know what they all think? They think I have sold the house and got pots of money! My elder sister Elisa's son is broadcasting this news to the world. And this Jessie,—she has taken leave from her bank and is camping here to conduct an enquiry!" said Tony, fisting his palm to show his resolve.

"I am not afraid of any one!" Thrusting his chest forward and flailing his arms, Tony said, "The builder gives me just one flat. . . . . That is all,—a two bedroom flat. I have, after all, three children. That is the minimum I need. I can't settle for a smaller flat so that I can distribute the rest of the compensation among my sisters,—no! I am no Saint!

"Last week Elisa's husband and the eldest son had come. They said, 'this and that' in their military style and left. Now this Jessie! She says I have received lot of money and I am not letting out the truth. She thinks I am well off as it is. What does she know about my troubles?" He asked rhetorically, "You know how things are with me. Don't you? Yes or no,—tell me man!

"Anyway, the flat is for mother, who owns the house. And it is me who is looking after her. Have they considered it?—They simply want to grab something,—that is all!

"The other day Vakola uncle's son had come here for arbitration;—Jessie had asked him to come. The way he was talking,—Hey! Hey! . . . . He runs with the hare and hunts with the hound!"

Vincent's mind wandered off to the day he had fallen down from a large Mango tree during the days he was staying in Carvallho Villa as a kid. He felt sad that some among the people who were associated with this memory were no longer living and others have changed beyond recognition. Philip, who had run to him where he had fallen and taken him into the house was now dead,—so was uncle Gregory who had made solicitous enquiries after returning from work in the evening; Aunt Sophie who had applied balm to the swelling on his forehead has become a wreck,—and the mischievous but essentially innocent boy who had playfully pulled at his leg and caused him to fall,—had morphed into a potbellied greedy man with no traces of any scruples. Vincent was on the verge of sighing, just when he suddenly realized that the mango tree did not exist anymore.

"Hey, Tony,—What ever happened to that mango tree, *yar*!" he yelled involuntarily, pointing to the place where he remembered it was.

"The mango tree . . . . ? Oh, yes! We cut it down . . . . Also the four coconut trees at the back, the jackfruit tree at the entrance, two *chikkoo* trees . . . . I think we had to cut down most of them. The damn trees were fouling with the building plan everywhere, man!"

True enough, Vincent realized upon looking around, that most of the trees had gone and the place had taken on a barren look.

Tony warmed up to the subject,—"Vincent, you know what?—Just one injection, man, you inject it near the root and within four days . . . . *Khallas*! . . . . Finished!"

Tony's eyes shone with the recollection of his triumph over the trees. "You don't have to bother anymore. The leaves go dry and fall and the tree shrivels literally. Then you don't feel bad cutting the tree . . . . And no bother from municipality or the stupid Tree-lovers, when you cut down a dead tree."

Vincent failed to react.

Dora, emerging from behind one of the piles, asked plaintively, "Did nobody object when you felled the trees?"

"Yes ma'am, they did." Tony said jumping two steps forward. "That D'Souza, Philip's friend,—he alone is enough. He did come, and standing upright like a preacher, tried to lecture me. I didn't care. I said—don't poke your nose in other's affairs. You try any trouble here and I'll fix you up. I said that. He started, if only Philip were alive, and I said,—So? Philip is no more, so what do we do about it? Then he slunk away quietly."

"See, it is not me who is felling the trees. Having given the plot to the builder, what have I got to do with it? On top, if you ask me, the trees were not felled,— they died,—and it can be proved! You know,—all these fellows come preaching,—but when it comes to them, it is different. This very D'Souza, when two of the trees in his own compound were felled, the bloke did nothing. And he writes to papers. Just because he has a pen in his hand, can he write any nonsense he wants?" Tony's eyes had bulged and face flushed.

Dora regretted having raked up the topic.

As the couple managed to take leave of Tony and came out to the Turner Road, Dora said, "I think your cousin was drunk."

"Drunk or sober,—he is the same." said Vincent dismissively.

How could they have ripped away those lovely, pale yellow, wooden lattices? And what would they have done with them?

Dora suggested that they go to the Jogger's Park at the end of the road and Vincent nodded. Just as they were to enter the park, someone called Vincent from behind and when they turned they saw Jessie, briskly walking towards them from the Chimbai end of the road.

"Let us go into the park. I have got to talk to you." said Jessie earnestly.

Jessie was the youngest of the Carvallho siblings. Vincent noticed that Jessie still had that catch in her voice. When she spoke, couple of words would tumble out while the words behind them would get caught in her throat, and as they piled up, her throat would swell,—till all the words caught up in her throat spilled out in a heap.

Since it was a holiday, the Jogger's park was crowded. When the trio reached the western edge of the park and sat down on a concrete seat, the sun had already set. The sea had receded, leaving a few puddles among the rocks, which caught the residual light of the western horizon. The forlorn looking patches of mangroves, which grew at the edge of the sea, had trapped any number of plastic bags, fluttering in the breeze.

The three sat there talking, as the cool wind blowing from the west caressed them.

"What did Tony tell you?" Jessie asked directly.

"Meaning . . . ? . . . . Oh! . . . Nothing much. The house . . . . It was only today . . . ." Vincent.

"Tony is very clever, you know. We realized it only when they started the demolition. If Philip were alive today, do you think all these things would have happened? And mother has gone senile. The house is in shambles. And Tony? Just not bothered, so casual and shameless . . . . If you spit out the hot *ghee*, you waste it and if you gulp it, the throat is scalded." Jessie sighed.

"Tony doesn't have a proper job, you know. They sacked him along with so many others,—gave them provident fund, compensation and all. It suits him fine. He is acting big in front of those workers.

"Yesterday night he came home punch-drunk. And the way he was yelling and screaming, waking up the neighbourhood, just because I tried to reason with him. He was shaking all over and saying,—you get out right now and take mother with you."

Lowering her voice Jessie asked, "Did he tell you anything?"

Vincent was lost in thoughts and Dora said, "No."

Jessie explained many things,—how 'the Saldana fellow the lawyer, is giving him all the crooked ideas', how 'Tony had booked a *Contessa* Car, all the while claiming that he has no money on him,' and things like that.

"Let him buy an aeroplane if he wants, I wouldn't grudge that. But why tell so many lies? If only mother had been alright, all these things would not have happened." Jessie wiped her tears.

Vincent suddenly asked her, "Say Jessie, what you think has happened to all those lovely wooden lattices and the stained glass panel?"

Jessie answered hotly, "What else? He would have torn them and thrown them away. You think he values such things?" and then toning down, Jessie added, "But now that you asked me, I thought I saw pieces of them on a heap at the back of the house. But if you so much as enquire about it, Tony is sure to say that—Vincent is asking for his share."

Jessie continued, "Come to think of it, you also may be entitled to have a share, Vincent, through your mother. After all it was grandfather who had bought the land."

There was an awkward silence now and nobody spoke any further.

Jessie shortly got up and left.

Vincent and Dora continued to sit and stare as darkness gathered over the Arabian Sea.

IN THRALL TO A MELODY

The asphalt road was burning hot in the high noon.

Harshita was crossing the road holding her little son's hand. Not yet used to her new shoes with extra high heels, which she had bought yesterday, her legs seemed to tangle with each other. The earrings, also new, were so large that they swung as she walked briskly and struck her cheeks rhythmically. She wore a light pink chiffon sari with blouse of matching hue having embroidered designs on its sleeves. As she turned to look back briefly after crossing the road, her darting eyes seemed to seek something.

Harshita Parekh lived in an apartment on the third floor of 'Swapna', a building in Bombay's northern suburb of Borivili. Her son's school-bus stopped on the other side of the road right in front of the building.

She helped her son board the school bus, and handed him the water bottle. She greeted familiar faces among other women who had collected there to see their wards off with Hi-Hellos, nods or just smiles, till the bus left, and then, hailing a three-wheeled auto-rickshaw, got into it, muttering something to the effect of being in a hurry. Even after she left, the fragrance that was in the sweep of her sari's fluttering free end spread and enveloped those who were in its wake, and induced in them—unaware—a high that lasted for a long time.

—I felt as if I saw him just as I was helping the child get into the bus. I am sure it was he, my stalker, who was behind the tree, wearing a blue shirt. I know I shouldn't have looked at him. He was looking at me like he wanted to swallow me. I can only hope I'd never come under the spell of those eyes.

These thoughts electrified her, but on the other hand, anger mounted against him within. She had always been tormented by these mixed up reactions.

Her mind suddenly changed tracks and got engaged in imagining how she looked in her light pink chiffon sari, and the image she made of herself thrilled her. It was her favourite past time to imagine how she looked at any given time—and it never failed to excite her. She was aware that her good looks attracted people around her, and she was proud of it. But at the same time, it tickled her to pretend that she was unaware of the attention she was getting or to pretend that she didn't care about it; and the art of both such pretentions had been perfected by her.

On her round face was a dark beauty spot on the right cheek, and just below that formed an elongated dimple when she smiled. She let her long tresses fall freely on her back, restrained only by two tresses picked from behind the ears and tied at the back of her head with a clip. A few strands of hair from above her forehead reached down to her cheeks and were left free to sway.

After she sat in the *rickshaw*, Harshita stuck her head out and looked back apprehensively and then snapping back to the position of facing the front, she sat stiffly.

—Why is he following me? He is really annoying me. But my eyes seeking him out is even more annoying. It is disgusting!

She sometimes got so upset with her ways that, in the manner of punishing herself for her indiscretions, she would neglect herself utterly, not even bothering to dress or groom herself properly. She would then look so ordinary and inconspicuous that it became hard for people who knew her to recognize her. Wearing a voile sari hugging her body, her hair unruly and face oily, she would come to the bus stop with a look of great detachment from the world. She would wait for the school bus standing aloof, her back resting against a nearby tree and her eyes fixed on the infinite.

It was impossible to categorize Harshita Parekh into any type. When she talked—she talked too much—or else she clammed up and remained aloof. One day she would be interested in everything from cinema to theatre to parties, and hop from one topic to another animatedly. But the very next day she would be very dejected and display utter disinterest in those very things, and might even say—'who needs them?'

She rarely mixed with her neighbours. In fact, there was an ever-present hint in her behaviour that the place and the environs she lived in did not come up to her standards. Once while talking to Harini, one of her very few friends in the neighbourhood, Harshita did concede that she felt constrained in that locality and that she doubted if she was ever meant to live in such a place.

In her talks, there were frequent references to . . . . 'Living among these people', 'for these people . . . .' or 'the mind-set of these people is such'—making it amply clear that she, instead of living among her equals, was, by fault living among those much below her status. But it was not that she looked down upon the people of her locality or ignored them—she loved them; a love borne of compassion for her fellow residents, the kind of love one felt while atop a hill for people who were seen below, or the love one had for plants, trees and animals because all were part of one grand unified world of many life forms.

She did interact with others in the locality but with a sublime detachment, even as her behaviour betrayed the regret she had of spending her days with 'commoners'.

She often felt that the place she lived was not the real Bombay at all. But, for that matter, many residents of South Bombay did harbour such opinion about the suburbs of North Bombay; for them Bombay meant places like Fort, Cuff parade, Malabar Hill, or at the most Worli-Seaface, and their most liberal interpretation of Bombay might extend it up to Dadar or Shivaji Park, but under no circumstances would it extend to the wilderness beyond those boundaries.

Harshita was born in Walkeshwar, a part of Malabar Hill, where her parents lived in a building on the road that ran in front of the famous Jain Mandir. She grew up with all the privileges of a prosperous household in a posh locality like Malabar Hill, and it included lots of fun like going to parties, picnics, movies, beaches or eating in fancy restaurants or at quaint street-food stalls,—all these with lots of friends, privileged and spirited like her. So, it was quite a change for her when she came to live in the quiet and uneventful place like Borivili and she became like—what else—fish out of water. The drastic change from the carefree life of an unmarried young woman to the sedate and restricted life of a married woman was in itself too much for her, but to add to the confusion, she thought it was in reality a part of the problems of relocating to the distant Borivili, and this explained her prejudices and the blame Borivili had to take consequently for her woes.

Kumar was selected by her parents as husband for her, but she married him only after she had liked him without any reservation. When he had come to her house with his parents to see her for the first time, she had found him very attractive in dark blue pants and full sleeved, cream-coloured shirt. Later when they sat together and talked, she found the fragrance of the perfume he wore very alluring, winning her heart and mind. Kumar, being in the business of selling movies to exhibitors, had talked at length to Harshita about cinema and actors he knew, and she had found him very interesting and his talk highly stimulating.

Kumar's parents were in Ahmedabad and his only sister was already married, and so Harshita's mother was rightly happy that her daughter would not have to bother about in-laws or running a large household, and she had told Harshita so—that it would be a hassle-free wedded life for her. As for Harshita's father, the fact that his would-be son-in-law owned a flat in Borivili and, what is more, had even booked a new Fiat car, was all that mattered, and it had excited him greatly. Of course, to own both an apartment and a new car was the ultimate achievement for any young man in the nineteen eighties, considering the fact that no bank was then allowed to give loans for such profligacies by the government which believed in the virtues of utter austerity for its subjects.

The days following the engagement were very eventful and exciting. For both Harshita and Kumar, the fun filled year between the engagement and wedding went so fast as to be blurry. It had, in fact, become a practice, not only in their family but in their community as well, for the betrothed couple to have fun as much as possible before their wedding. So, Harshita and Kumar moved like quicksilver all over the city, having non-stop fun, as if there was no tomorrow. Harshita's grandma, who had been casting a disdainful eye on this new-fangled practice of her community's engaged couples, commented wryly that it appeared that the couple were pre-empting their entire life's outings in that just one year.

Every weekend, Harshita and Kumar, as if participating in some kind of a competition, would breathlessly go around seeking fun—typically, a movie in Eros, a comic play in Bhaidas Theatre, eating *bhelpuri* in Chowpati, and finally an hour of contemplative time together amidst the rocks of Bandstand.

Kumar had once asked Harshita before they were engaged, when they were together in the Hanging Gardens for an evening out, if she liked movies. Harshita had responded with a resounding 'Yes', and consequently, Kumar had used his contacts and influence in Bollywood so that the two could attend many premiere shows or 'first-day-first-shows' In such major Cinemas as Plaza, Eros, Maratha Mandir and Regal. If they went to a movie at Plaza, dinner would be at Copper Chimney or if the movie was in Regal or Sterling, they would eat in Status or go to Chowpati Beach for its famous junk-food.

It was during one such outing in Chowpati, as they were eating *bhelpuri*, that Kumar had asked her, 'Does it bother you that you will have to move to Borivili?'

The novelty of his companionship, the magic in the air of the beach, the mounting curiosity about the future wedded life,—all had combined or conspired to make her shake her head, indicating that it did not bother her at all.

'You know, it is only one hour by an express local train to Borivili from Churchgate Station' he has said to assure her.

After moving to Borivili, Harshita realized that although it took just one hour to reach Borivili, starting from the nearby Churchgate Station—that one hour meant a totally different world. The difference between Walkeshwar and Borivili was not just at the surface, but was deep down where it evoked a corrosive feeling of having sunk into a pit. Eventually Kumar sensed this feeling of his wife and used to console her, 'Let us have some money. Then we can move to Andheri.' But not only Andheri was no Walkeshwar—only a little nearer to it—but buying an apartment there was easier said than done, the prices there being more than double of those prevailing in Borivili.

The marriage put an effective end to all that wandering around the town in pursuit of pleasure. The pressure of work on Kumar increased substantially. For one, he had to catch up with the work he had put off for the many celebrations at the time of wedding, and secondly, the volume of his business had almost doubled within a few months of marriage. In fact, her relatives said that Harshita had brought luck to her husband, and such compliments had pleased Harshita and made her feel proud. But the flip side of this luck was that Kumar started coming home late at irregular hours, and travelled much more than before on business to places like Pune, Nagpur or Aurangabad. Harshita had to get used to spending time alone at home.

Kumar felt bad for his wife since he knew she was used to a life with parents, siblings and grandparents in a bustling house and that she would find it hard to be alone at home most of the time. To compensate for that, once in a while, he would hand her a couple of thousand rupees to spend as she liked. With that money, Harshita would go for shopping with her sister or friends and sometimes even alone, to buy things like clothes, bangles or hand bags for herself and derive some strange satisfaction from it. On Harshita's shopping habits, Kumar's sister, Poorvi, used to joke that one could do some window shopping just by looking at what Harshita brought home after her shopping expeditions. Compared to the love and care Kumar was lavishing on her, Harshita felt it was a small sacrifice to make on her part to live in the boring suburb of Borivili and bear the loneliness at home. After Harshita became pregnant, Kumar was loathe to leave her alone at home, and so, promptly got his mother, who was in Ahmadabad, to come and live in his house to provide his wife care and companionship. This eased his guilt and enabled him to get much more involved in his business that was already growing rapidly.

It was the time when major transformations were taking place in the field of Kumar's business. Because of the increasing popularity of recorded videos, cinema houses were closing down, and it was thought that cinema's days would be numbered. But then suddenly large malls started to come up all over, and with them came multiplexes with big appetite for movies. Kumar's business surged and he was now so successful in it that he made enough money to double the size of his apartment by buying and joining the one adjoining his. Harshita's people said that though she had to move to the distant suburbs, the disadvantage was more than compensated by her stars being in ascendency, bringing so much of prosperity and progress.

Even after Harshita's delivery, her mother-in-law continued to live with her son's family in Borivili, except for occasional visits to Ahmedabad. But during such time when his mother was away, Kumar would ensure that his sister Poorvi came to live with them to provide companionship to Harshita. Whenever Kumar asked her, 'Are you getting bored?' Harshita, though despondent with no real control on her feelings, would vehemently deny it. As her son grew up and started going to school, Harshita became busy with his schooling—like taking him to the school bus, getting him back and helping him with his studies. But her intermittent feeling of despondency had increased in frequency.

About this time, she had begun to visit her neighbourhood friend Harini for a chat whenever her feeling of gloom became too intense to bear, and such visits made her feel better. The two were in the same class in Xavier's College at one time, and now, not only were they neighbours but their sons went to the same school; all these had brought them close now.

The two had lost touch after their marriages, but found each other one day at the school-bus-stop when Harini recognized her college-classmate and hesitatingly asked her, 'Aren't you Harshita?'

At that time, Harshita, who, as was her wont sometimes, was standing aloof, holding her son's hand and resting her back against the trunk of a tree—indifferent to the world, eyes focussed on the beyond.

Upon being addressed by Harini, Harshita had perked up instantly like a deflated balloon leaping into fullness when inflated. Overjoyed, she took Harini's both hands in hers tightly and exclaimed, 'Hi! Harini, how come you are here?'

The excitement in Harshita's voice was such that heads turned to stare at the two friends with great curiosity. Harini was happy when she was greeted with such effusion, but was surprised too, for she had only a nodding acquaintance with Harshita in the college and was by no means close to her.

In the college days, Harshita easily stood out among the students, being a good looking, lively girl who always dressed attractively. She used to shine in many college events like 'Talents Day' or 'Inter colligate

Competition', but most of all, in the annual cultural event 'Malhar' for which students from other colleges of Bombay also thronged, sometimes—it was said— just to hear and see Harshita sing. She was the kind of girl whom everyone seemed to know; energetic and talented, moving in a circle of similar girls determined to be active all the time. For someone like Harini, who was not quite the outgoing type, it was not easy to break into that charmed circle; she was not even on its periphery. But the changed circumstances brought the two together now.

Harshita's desire to sing had not dimmed in the years since her college days. Even when she chatted with her friend, Harshita would hum, and sometimes stop talking altogether to sing snatches of songs in a very mellow voice, appearing to let her mind float in a reverie. There were times, even while walking on the road, when she would cut herself off from her environs and immerse herself in a melody that was playing within her—so totally that, seized by emotions, her eyes would swell with tears.

As their friendship grew, one day Harini had urged her friend, 'Harshita, sing for me, it has been so long since I heard you sing.'

Harshita showed some reluctance initially, 'No! My voice is not what it used to be.' But Harini had persisted till her friend relented and sang for her. Later on, it became normal for Harshita to sing whenever she met Harini in her apartment, sometimes even without her prompting.

Harshita mostly sang sentimental movie-songs of the late seventies, originally sung by the likes of Mukhesh and Geeta Dutt. She seemed to invest those old songs with fresh life, deeply feeling for the lyrics and pouring herself into the melody with such intensity that sometimes tears rolled down her cheeks and sobs punctuated the lines.

During one such musical soiree at Harini's apartment, Harshita, sitting on the edge of the bed, her back resting against the bed post, was singing a romantic song. As was typical of such movie-songs, its lyrics expressed the feelings of a lady towards her lover—how she regretted falling in love with him and felt like being infected with a decease with no cure.

Harini took it up to tease Harshita, 'Wait, Kumar will come running to you to grab you and provide the badly needed cure.'

Harshita retorted, 'Fat chance! He is in Nagpur . . . and even if he were here, the song would have fallen on deaf ears.'

She had then promptly started another romantic song in which a lady implores her lover with the most common 'come hither' line . . . 'Come my love, take me in your arms . . .'

To Harini, the whole room seemed to be in thrall to Harshita's melodious voice, while the latter's languid posture, expression of great abandon, and the throaty voice—all seemed to suggest that Harshita was being passionately in love with herself.

The next day evening, Harshita came to Harini's apartment again, and going straight to the window that overlooked the road in front of the building, she looked down through the window, and then quickly drew the curtains. Standing against the wall, Harshita whispered dramatically, 'You don't know Harini! I made a mistake by singing here yesterday. You know the window was open then, and I think he was down there below near the gate, listening to my singing.' Harshita's eyes clearly showed signs of sleeplessness.

Not comprehending, Harini asked her friend, 'Who heard?'

I think it was when I was coming out of I-Max Cinema that I saw him for the first time—wasn't it? Yes, I am sure about it—and that was the day the feeling of being followed began.

Four or five days after her sister Choti's betrothal, the whole family had been to a movie theatre with Choti's fiancé. Harshita's mind for some reason wasn't on the movie. In addition, Kumar had not come with her to the movie; he had rushed to Aurangabad on some urgent business after telling her, 'Sorry Harshi . . . Can't make it. But you know if you go it is as good as both of us going . . . You have always made good for both of us.'

Meanwhile, in the theatre, Choti and her fiancé were smiling and exchanging glances, reminding Harshita of the happy days she and Kumar had spent together after their engagement. It excited her even now to recall how her fiancé had been utterly captivated by her scintillating dance at her cousin's pre-wedding celebration of *mehndi* which the two had attended right after their engagement She too had been captivated by him—Kumar was good looking those days—handsome and in good shape and was at his charming best that day.

It was only in the recent past that Kumar had become plump, with his bloated face hiding its handsome features. Cinema, parties, meetings, tea-coffee and snacks at any time of the day—all these had caused the damage and Kumar himself now regretted it. But what use regretting? But then, as he said, he couldn't help the city life or the ways of his business. That might be so—thought Harshita—but the fact was that fun had gone out of the marriage.

She could not at all follow the story of the movie that day. She had given up.

Later in the theatre's cafeteria—it was when all of us were eating 'makki ka roti & sarson ka saag'—that I saw him properly. He looked like the actor Shah-Rukh-Khan with his rumpled hair and deep dimples. He was sitting at a table at some distance, with a tall glass of juice in his hand, staring at me without batting an eye lid. It was so irritating. But I thought it best to ignore him.

She was not new to getting appreciative glances; she had got used to it right from the early years of her youth. Not only she was good looking but she knew how to dress and act to attract attention—she had mastered this technique when in college, and it had become a habit with her since then. Now, the practice of acting at all times, as if to attract someone, had become so ingrained in her as to seem natural. The way she stood—with a sideways bend in the middle, with her hand on her hip, or the way she walked with a swing or turned abruptly—had all the marks of a model on the ramp.

That day I had worn a light green salwar and a sleeveless kameez. I had swung my finely embroidered yellowish green shawl over my shoulder as I walked over to the ice-cream counter, and the young man with the tall glass of juice in his hand had continued to stare at me. Not only that, he had a smile on his face flaunting familiarity. And when I had reached out to receive the ice cream cone, he was right behind me and later when I was paying the bill, his hand was so close that it just missed touching mine.

As she returned to her table, Choti and her fiancé were still laughing as if the others did not exist for them. It was too much for Harshita. She had then called her sister aside and whispered in her ear, 'Look! That fellow over there has been staring at me ever since I walked into this place . . . . and is following me wherever I go. It is all very, very, embarrassing for me. This is too much!'

Choti had asked rather nonchalantly, 'Who? Where?' and was quite dismissive, 'Nobody is there! I don't see anyone!' After that, she had held my hand and pulled me away, without really bothering about the matter. On the one hand it was awkward for me to point my finger at that fellow, and on the other, I felt bad that this girl had all her attention fixed on her fiancé and had no concern for me at all.

Harshita, standing against the wall that day at Harini's place, had continued, 'I am afraid he liked my singing yesterday'

And she added with sadness, 'He is virtually shadowing me'

Then, she said, 'He is so mad after me . . .' and sighed.

She shuddered as she continued, 'Oh God! What will I do if my husband or his people come to know?'

The dark rings below her eyes seemed to become darker when she said—'Harini, what shall I do? Nothing occurs to me!' and the last sentence was uttered in such hurry that it was almost swallowed before it came out of her.

Harshita went back to the window, pulled the curtain and after peeping out briefly, she swiftly drew the curtain back and fell back into the sofa. Covering her eyes with her cupped hands, she groaned, 'He is still there!'

But, by the time Harini went to the window to see for herself, that man had gone away. She did not see anyone near the gate or under the nearby *neem* tree.

After this incident, whenever she met Harshita, the latter would invariably come up with a complaint about him—like he invited her to a movie, or that, during the celebration of the Navaratri festival he had pressed her to go with him to the nine-day-dancing event of her community. She rued, 'Harini, he does not understand that it wouldn't be proper for me to go out with him like that. Why is he harassing me in this manner? . . . . and I am afraid somehow I am at fault.'

And every time Harshita came with complaints of such harassment, Harini had tried to console her. Harini also suggested she could inform her husband and complain to the police about it, but Harshita turned down the suggestions always, saying it would only make matters worse for her by raising suspicions.

Once by mistake, Harini told her that she should not do anything that might indirectly encourage that person.

Harshita was indignant, 'Harini, how can you imagine me encouraging him in any way?' Having said that, Harshita promptly began to blame herself, 'Harini am I encouraging him . . . Have I fallen so low?'

Once, she said, the man had rolled up his shirt sleeve and thrust his arm forward to show the tattoo on his forearm. She had been shocked to read the letterings—I LOVE YOU HARSHITA.

'Poor fellow . . . . It must have hurt him so much!' she said to Harini, and the twinkle in her eyes revealed the thrill she felt because so much pain had been endured by him for her sake.

The very next moment, Harshita's face fell and she said with pain, 'I have repeatedly appealed to him and reasoned with him, that I am after all a married woman. But he didn't relent at all . . . . and you know what he said?'

Harini became curious, but Harshita seemed to hold within her whatever he had said, as if to keep savouring it.

Finally it came out, 'He said to me— Harshita! . . . Is love something that one summons? It just blossoms in the heart on its own.' The tremors of excitement in her voice said it all.

Once when I was at 'Shoppers' Stop' with Harini, trying on some earrings in front of a mirror, I thought I heard someone saying,—'It suits you well'. When I turned to look, it was the same fellow—the same Shahrukh— hairstyle, mellow smile and the same unfathomed depth in his eyes. He had both his hands in the pockets of his pants and as he stared at me, the look in his eyes said that we had known each other for a long, long time.

'Oh my God . . . ! How do I escape from this man?' I said to myself when I turned away to try another earring,

and he tells me—unbelievably—'No! The first one was better'. Either it was the appeal of his eyes or the affection in his voice—whatever the reason—it made me smile. Or it seemed the smile forced itself on me.

Later I have cursed myself many a time for that smile.

While at the cash counter, Harshita had pinched Harini's hand and pointed at him. But Harini couldn't find where he was. She went around the counter and even went to the section selling earrings, but couldn't find him. Apparently she took it as a challenge and went right up to the exit to look for him. Harini wondered if her friend was simply having delusions.

When Harini returned after making, what she thought was a very thorough search for the man, Harshita, standing with the shopping bag in her hand, had looked right through Harini and asked her in a tired, lifeless voice, 'Couldn't you find him?'

A few days later, one Saturday afternoon, Harshita came with her son to Harini's place, seemingly in great hurry, and after assigning Harini the responsibilities of putting her son aboard the school bus, had left the place immediately, leaving behind her son with his school bag and water-bottle. Dressed in a long silk gown and a silk blouse reaching down to her hip—both dark red with brocaded green borders—her eyes smartly lined and hair bound loosely by a cloth band, Harshita had looked dramatically different to Harini.

Surveying her Harini had said, 'You look like a college beauty that you were one time.'

Delicately brushing aside a tress that had strayed over her eye with the tip of her index finger, and tilting her head coyly, Harshita had protested, 'Don't tell me!'

While leaving hurriedly, her silk dress rustling, Harshita had said vaguely that she was off to a party thrown by some Bollywood people.

But Harini was left wondering as to where really her friend was going to, for she remembered Harshita telling her as they were coming out of Shoppers-Stop after the previous week's incident that the man who has been stalking her had offered to take her to 'Jazz by the Bay', a seaside place on Marine Drive, where fashionable young people came to eat, drink and dance.

'Are you going to that disco? . . . it's so far!' Harini remembered saying, to which she had reacted with some degree of indignation, 'No way . . . Harini, am I crazy to take his offer!' But all the same her eyes seemed to sparkle and dance in anticipation.

Just a few days later, when Harini met her friend as usual at the school-bus-stop, she was in a different avatar, wearing a faded *salwar-Kameez,* and a crumpled *dupatta* over that. Her ears, neck, forehead were all bereft of any adornment and she wore no makeup or decorative mark on her forehead. Harshita said 'Hi' to her without any enthusiasm and then turned to look elsewhere.

After the bus left with their wards on it, Harini could not help asking Harshita, 'Why this monastic attire? Looks your hair hasn't seen a comb for a long time now.'

Harshita simply said, 'Let go' and brushed her hair with her hand distractedly.

Next day, it was Harshita's mother-in-law who came with the boy to see him aboard the school bus and told Harini that her daughter-in-law was not well when asked about her.

Harshita was gradually becoming withdrawn and unconcerned about everyday life like cooking or even looking after her child. She would sit cross-legged for hours on the extended window sill of her bedroom or in the swinging wicker-chair that hung in a corner, and it became her mother-in-law's responsibility to run the household.

Later, when Harini went to meet her, she asked her, 'Harini, is it a sin to love somebody?'

Despite her mother-in-law and Poorvi trying to cheer her up, Harshita would complain bitterly, 'I am finished . . . I know what people are saying behind my back'

Her mother-in-law had protested, 'Why do you say such things? It is so inauspicious! You are perfectly all right', but these words had no effect at all on her.

Harshita eventually became scared to even step out of her house. She had become so distrustful of people that when she saw them on the road, she suspected that they were talking about her and laughing at her. Kumar and others tried to convince and console her, 'Harshita, no one is talking about you . . . it is all your imagination.'

They say I am imagining things . . . how I wish it was true. No, it is not my imagination. It is your delusion about my innocence—that's what it is.

Poorvi, who consoled her overtly, also said at her back, 'God knows what indiscretions she had done when in college. Now it is all coming back!'

Kumar took her to a doctor for consultation, who prescribed her sleeping pills and some medicines for lowering her blood pressure. Her mother-in-law had to remind Harshita to take the medicines regularly and sometimes she even had to personally administer them to her on time.

Eventually when Harshita practically stopped coming out of her room, the long endearing letters started coming to her.

I hide them in the cupboard . . . . but within the folds of my sari. But still the words in the letters torment me.

'Harshita I am forever thinking about you, how can I live without you?

'I passionately love everything about you, the way you walk, stand . . . . even the things you have touched . . . . or just anything that has been hallowed by your association.'

I read the letters sitting in the swing-chair and my mind becomes light as the petals of a flower. That young man, as if he has nothing else to do, goes rapturously into such minute details about me . . . right from my toes to the curly tresses that caress my cheeks . . . . On top he insists, 'Come with me just one time . . . please . . . just once . . . to Chowpati Beach!'

Yes! Chowpati Beach . . . Kumar has worn his dark blue T-shirt and I am in my faded light blue jeans and an orange top. His ruffled hair and my curly forelocks are blowing in the wind . . . I am standing with Kumar at the edge of the water, just where the distant waves are breaking and washing my feet . . . .

Now we are sitting on the sand drinking water from the same coconut with two straws . . . our eyes in each other's and the time has stood still—like in a photograph.

I remember those days, it is as if nothing else has happened in my life since then and that is all my memory is.

After their marriage, she used to tell Kumar—
occasionally at least—'Let us go to Chowpati Beach,
like we used to'

But years had rolled on quickly—too quickly for
Kumar to seize a moment that he could call theirs, and
before they knew they had been married already for ten
years. And that, of course, was celebrated grandly.

Kumar had presented a lovely diamond necklace
to Harshita to celebrate ten years of their married life.
He had gifts for everyone in the household. There was a
festive atmosphere in the house and Harshita had been
overwhelmed by it all.

That day too Harshita had suggested to Kumar—
that they go to Chowpati together one evening, and
Kumar had said, 'Why Chowpati?—we will go to
Singapore, Harshi! Let this busy year be over . . . so
many movies being released and my competitors
out to grab my business, I can't afford to relax now.
Chowpati . . . . well, It has to wait for us'—he laughed,
and Harshita also laughed—rather too heartily.

*I had not wanted to disappoint Kumar. He has been
working so hard—day and night—for me—for his son . . .
for all of us. My hand went to my new necklace and I felt
reassured of his love and was contented caressing it.*

Her aunt used to tell her, 'You are lucky
Harshita, . . . a husband like Kumar with no bad habits
at all—drinking, smoking or gambling . . . nothing . . .
doesn't even chew *paan* . . . forget about that which
hurts a woman most!'

So true . . . I know how rare it is to find men without bad habits. More than that, I feel so proud of the depth of his love for me.

Harshita pressed the letter in her hand to her chest and closed her eyes.

As the waves broke on the beach, the foaming water sweeping under our feet and tingling them, we ran hand in hand . . . just for the fun . . . the mind was carefree . . . . lots of laughter and running . . . . as the wind swept my face, my hair was flying madly . . . wave after wave—I was begging Kumar—wait, one more wave—no more after this—one, last one please—Kumar is running with his arm around me—and it is a huge, gigantic candy floss . . . . both of us are eating it face to face . . . . but I can't see Kumar's face . . . because it is so huge . . . now melting as the tongue touches it and its sweetness intoxicating . . . . with half closed eyes I am savouring it . . . . as we relish it, the candy is shrinking and now I can see the face—his face—other man's face . . . but where is Kumar?, . . . I see only the other face. What if I open my eyes fully—?

Harshita got up from the swing-chair as if on an impulse, went to the basin, splashed water on her face. Even as her eyes filled up with tears, she washed her face with soap, washing away the unstoppable tears from her eyes. Drying her face with a towel she looked into the mirror and saw a face with puffed up eyes looking at her piercingly. Once again, like going back into a cocoon, she went and settled in the swinging wicker-chair.

All the troubles because of those letters . . . . I should get rid of them . . . What if someone's eyes fall on them. But . . . I don't seem to have the strength in my hands to shred them.

Suddenly she got up from the wicker-chair, went to the cupboard in her room and picking up all the letters from it, put them into her hand bag and went out of her apartment.

Harshita, who was at the door of Harini's apartment with unkempt hair and puffed up eyes, thrust all the letters into her friend's hand as soon the door was opened by her, and said, 'Look here, I am going mad reading these letters from him. Keep them with you.'

And continuing she said, 'See! See for yourself what all he writes. You wouldn't believe!'

Harini, having run her eyes on the topmost letter, stood staring at the small bundle of letters in her hand and her eyes then shifted to Harshita's face. She stood gazing at Harshita's face, as thoughts raced through her mind—'What is the matter with this girl? Aren't these letters in her own handwriting? Why is she complaining after writing these letters to herself?'

What she saw of Harshita disturbed her. Uncombed hair that had lost its lustre, eyes devoid of their sparkle, the sunken cheeks where dimples once formed—she wondered if it is the same lively Harshita she knew.

That day, Kumar had finally decided to admit her to a specialized hospital for psychiatric treatment, but when he was ready to take her, she adamantly refused to go with him.

'I am not going anywhere! Nothing is wrong with me . . . . I am perfectly normal.' she insisted and refused to get up from the wicker-chair.

Poorvi, who had come to help, was continuously making asides like—'Why has a perfectly normal person been acting so weird all these days? Or is it a put on act now?'

Kumar kept chiding his sister, 'Poorvi can you please stop it!' But at the same time he found Harshita's adamant 'I won't come' very trying.

Couldn't he ask me to go with him to the beach . . . or hold my hand and take me to a 'Barista' and order a cappuccino and say to me, 'Let us sit here sipping coffee and let time wait!'

Harshita looked at his thinning hair and receding hairline, and said, 'I see a strand of white hair on your head. Let me pluck it.'

By then Kumar had given up on her and was already at the door. It was not clear what occurred to him all of a sudden. He came back to her and lowered his head to her, and as she was plucking the offending strand of silvery hair, he asked her, 'Harshi, shall we go to Chowpati Beach? Will you come with me?'

'Has he really said what I heard?'

Harshita wiped the tears with the back of her hand, and looked at him with clear eyes, and said, 'Let us go!'

She brushed her hair standing in front of the mirror, puffed it a bit and set it right. She carefully adjusted the *dupatta* over her chest—as if it was the shoulder band that Beauty-contestants wear across their chest with the participant country's name on it—and took her purse in her hand.

When they got off from the car, Harshita looked up at the sign board and said, 'Kumar, Where have you brought me to?'

THE SMALL GATE OF NAGAMMA'S HOUSE

'**One** would sooner miss the flowers on the temple-deity's crown' than this trio in the evenings who sat there chatting.

The small gate of Nagamma's house was at the edge of the roadside gutter. It was wide enough for one, or utmost, for two abreast and its height came up to one's waist. It had a crude clasp in the form of a loop of cord which was the object of Nagamma's daily heated argument with the maid, Anthi, who invariably overlooked to engage it with the post. And the open gate was,—what else, but an open invitation to the roaming cattle, which rushed in to make short work of the few remaining plants in a patch in the yard that passed for a garden.

It was not the practice to open the main gate, which was just a couple of feet away. It always remained closed, locked firmly. Anyway,—no sooner it was evening, you found Nagamma seated on the platform by the side of the small gate, one foot up, folded, and the other dangling, while her friend Puranamma squatted in front of her and the maid Anthi sat nearby, hunched on the low mound of the coconut tree. This was a daily sight.

"I don't know! They say it is raining. What kind of rain is this? When it rained,—well, it really rained—in olden times . . . you didn't see the sun for days!" That is how Nagamma might start,—something from the hoary past.

"Once when I was returning from father's house,—I was pregnant with Narayan then,—our boat was in mid-stream and what do we see? The sky had turned pitch black. And then it starts raining,—in torrents. The boatman says,—don't be afraid, and next thing he asks me, what do we do now? What could I say? And I had children with me,—Sarasu in my arms and the other little ones, one eight year old,—others, six and four." Her father had said why go alone, and had sent Joyisa's boy along with her. That boy's fretful screams, wild swaying of the boat, children being asked to bail out the water that was filling up with their cupped hands, later on,—spotting an islet and spending a whole night there after brushing aside the boatman's scare about the ghost tree on it with terse 'To hell with ghosts!' comment,—the story unwinds in great detail.

Mention of the awe-inspiring rains might provoke Puranamma to say with verve, her eyes flashing, "Nagamma, do you remember the deluge on my wedding day? Abba! It was a rain not of this world!"

Starting from the rains, the talk would meander any which way and then become a soliloquy from the depth of an anguished soul. Nagamma's tongue was sharp and direct. Smile was rare on her slightly buck-toothed face with a *kum-kum* dot between her eyebrows, pasted with gum. Her handful of remaining hair was combed severely and bound tightly into an oily knot. Come October, she would complete sixty three years of her life,—but her hair was all silvery already. 'Puranamma is seven years older than me,—but look at her charcoal-black hair!' she used to say to herself.

Puranamma's face was wide as a winnow with a rupee-coin-sized *kum-kum* dot on her forehead. Because of her high cheekbones, a smile seemed spread across her face permanently. Her uncontrollable curly tresses were plaited and then coiled into a bun on which she always wore flowers,—jasmine or chrysanthemums or if nothing else, *suragi* at least.

Puranamma was not her real name. Her parents had named her Bhagyavathi. When she had started to read out the *Puranas* in a ringing voice every Friday, sitting cross-legged in *Padmasana* on the veranda of her house, the book spread before her,—a regular audience comprising quite a few women of the neighbourhood had gradually materialized. That is how the name Puranamma stuck to her. Even when not in this *Purana* reciting mode, Puranamma had the habit of quoting from the scriptures at the drop of a hat during normal circumstances. Needless to say, the characters of Ramayana or Mahabharata regularly popped up during her talks without any advance notice. Apart from all this, she did the *pooja* on her own at home, offering vermilion to the deity. There was considerable demand for her sacred vermilion packets—the major client being none other than Anthi. She would ask for the sanctified *kum-kum*, to use as a charm for her child to get rid of fever, nightmare or evil eye, or even to heal a minor bruise.

When Nagamma spent her time at the gate chatting and arguing with Puranamma or sharing her feelings with Anthi, she used to feel a sense of consolation and peace swelling up inside. No reason was strong enough to miss this tryst with her friends. Though it appeared like rambling and compulsive chatting, it was a subconscious therapy session going on there.

In Puranamma's godly stories and their morals, Nagamma tried to drown her pain, and in the strands of Anthi's fiercely independent life, she lost herself willingly.

When there was no trace of Anthi even as that day was coming to an end, and when Puranamma said, 'May be her husband got drunk and thrashed her', Nagamma said to herself, 'That is it, she has let me down again.'

Last month it was so. When Anthi's husband came home drunk, a big quarrel had ensued and then he had beaten her up,—whereupon Anthi had seized the stick from his hand and had given it back to him in good measure, all of which resulting in her not turning up for work for next two days. Nagamma got upset remembering this. The idea of going to the cattle-shed herself in this failing light was quite depressing. No doubt, it was she who did this chore earlier. But since last two years she had assigned it to Anthi, when her back started getting seized by cramp while getting up after milking.

For that matter, Anthi was never known to be lazy. Short and rotund, she was tough as nails. Neatly tying up her knee-length hair into a big bun, tucking up the *palav* of her sari and pulling up the hem up to her knees, she was ready for a hard days labour,—never to look up from the work.

Mornings she worked at three houses,—Nagamma's, her neighbour *Tahishildar's* and then Janna Bhatta's house in the back lane, and afternoons were spent vending tender grass,—the big bundles of which she brought from *Bena* to sell in the town to contracted householders who kept milk cows. She would unburden herself of the grass bundles with an audible sigh of relief at Nagamma's house and then milk her cow, Somi. After that she permitted herself about half hour stop at Nagamma's gate, before rushing off to her home, a mile away.

Nagamma was never tired of complaining to Anthi about the ever-diminishing size of her grass bundles. "What Anthi, did you say it was a grass bundle,—I thought it was a bunch of beans!" she might say sarcastically and add, "And you think worms have got into my head that I would buy this stuff?"

But such arguments never prevented her from continuing to buy the grass from Anthi. A handful of grass meant a measure more of milk from Somi.

That apart, Nagamma was fascinated by Anthi's way of life—not bound by rules other than her own. Anthi earned her living and that of her children and hence was not too much concerned about her husband who lived apart. She had built her shack next to her mother's. Should the husband turn up, she didn't mind cooking for him. But she was not the one to beseech him for anything, or go by his decree.

To Nagamma and Puranamma, news of the town had to filter only through Anthi,—who just disgorged it for them every evening. And when the other two went on analysing the fresh news that has been brought to them, Anthi would listen with dumb wonderment,—as if she was hearing it for the first time.

Complementing the assembly of three, passers-by on the road would stop there for a while and add some spicy tit-bits. 'Lanky' Wachanna, whizzing past on his bicycle, would slow down,—without veering from his ramrod straight posture on the saddle,—stop abruptly, and get off from his bicycle to talk of a few worldly things as he held his bicycle like it was a small toy before riding off.

Once in a while, 'Lawyer's Driver' Kushta, on his way, would break some news. It was he who had given the news about Madhavi on the previous day. He appeared tired and was dragging his feet as he passed by, when Nagamma called him to say,—"Kushta, how is it going?" Kushta stopped, came to her, and resting his elbow on the post, started,—"What to say, things are tough." and then went on to tell how he had hurt himself in the leg while peeling a coconut, and before pushing off, also told them about Madhavi's visit to the Lawyer's office.

Madhavi, who worked at the *Taluk* office, used to pass in front of Nagamma's house twice every day. Though Nagamma or Puranamma had not got acquainted with her, she was a familiar face to them for several years now. Madhavi had become friendly with Sanjeeva, who worked in the same office and whose house was next to Janna Bhatta's. So they had seen her with him often, while passing on that road.

Nagamma was never amused when she saw them shaking with laughter as they walked,—seemingly at anything the other had to say. And when someone mentioned about this pair, she would say tersely,—"To hell with them, don't bother me!", but all the same would go into details about how they ribbed and giggled, or how they looked at each other with side long glances and finally finish the topic with a disparaging,—"Oh! . . . So pretentious!" Nagamma would say that this is not the way decent people behaved during her time. But, she never missed an opportunity to watch them as they passed in front of her house, even if it was the busy morning hour,—by dropping anything in hand to stand and stare. She found them fascinating in spite of herself, though at the end she might disgustedly say, 'what the times have come to!'

Later on, as intense discussion was taking place among the trio whether Madhavi and Sanjeeva would marry or not, the marriage had already taken place and soon a child was also born to them. The two of them continued to pass in front of the house, so absorbed in talking to each other that the world might well have not existed for them. There were times when the trio at Nagamma's gate wondered what could be the subjects for such unending talks between the two from morning till evening.

But recently, the timings of their going to work and returning had changed. They were rarely seen going together. Also Anthi had reported about constant quarrels at their home. Arguments with raised voices, and following that, sounds of the husband beating the wife and her screaming—were said to be heard by those at Janna Bhatta's house. Now the matter had reached the intense stage of divorce and Kushta had given the news of divorce notice being dispatched from the Lawyer's office.

After Kushta left, the talks at Nagamma's gate went round and round this fresh news. Puranamma, commented,—"Such exchanging of words is common in a marriage. But to leave the husband for that! Well times are such. But then, is there no consideration of children's tomorrow?"

The rhetoric question presumed the acceptance of her views by the other two. To boot it, she also quoted verses from the scripture,—how Krishna in *Dwapara Yuga* had described the evils of the impending Kali Yuga.

"Our husbands haven't exactly kept us in the lap of luxury, you know,"—said Nagamma in the manner of someone ready for a fight, looking away and planting her elbows on her knees to prop her chin.

"That's true Nagamma. What to say of the present generation? If they say horses have horns,—try correcting them! They are so adamant. One has to be patient,—especially a woman. Just see how patient was Sita-*mata*."

Mention of Sita-*mata*'s name raised the hackles of Nagamma. After all, was it right what Sita did? Is Sita going to be the sole example for ages to come?

Nagamma did not say it of course,—she couldn't offend Puranamma.

"The kind of hardships I had faced would have forced anyone else to jump into a river. But never did I beseech anyone,—mind you,"—said Nagamma, turning to them again and sweeping her hand for emphasis. Whom is she challenging,—Madhavi or Sita? Anthi and Puranamma just looked at her.

Nagamma sometimes wondered how so ever she managed a family of seven children, with a husband who led a jobless, empty life. It was more of anger than wonderment. If there was rice, there was no milk and if there was milk, there was no rice,—that is how it went. And the dummy of a husband was not even aware of the situation.

"But Nagamma, look at Sanjeeva's temerity,—beating her! What nonsense! Is that expected of an educated man?"—So saying Puranamma was groping for the names of those characters in the *Puranas* who had ruined themselves by their hubris and anger, when Anthi joined in, "Why! This is the kind of affair you'd expect in a community like mine."

"My husband had come very close to beating me once,"—Nagamma said suddenly, in a tone suggestive of strong determination to establish the fact that her misery was no less than Madhavi's. A trace of a smile seemed to have flickered in her eyes as she remembered the incident. It was just after the birth of Srinivasa. The second child, Sadananda, had high fever and was coughing so much that his lips hardly met. Who was to go to the doctor? Added to that, there was no money in the house, it was late in the night and there was no sign of her great husband.

No sooner the husband stepped into the house, she took it all on him,—"Wouldn't bother if you lost your child, would you? Don't know why I didn't go to my father's house for delivery though he did ask me,"—and more in that vein.

Quite unexpectedly he worked himself up to a great rage,—"Sick of always hearing about your father's house. Made a big mistake when I brought you from that snobbish, rich house." and so saying, had raised his hand to hit her.

"Beat me!"—She had screamed, and grabbing the sickle which lay in a corner and handing it to him, she had challenged him hysterically to finish her off,—"What mistake? What great things have you done for me?" She was toiling from morning till evening, whether pregnant or nursing a baby, and after all that she had to hear such things.

"You won't believe it,—there was never a time when he asked me,—if I needed anything or if I was tired. And about buying me a trinket of gold,—no, let us not talk about it,"—said Nagamma drawing a line of finality. Her eyes were flashing in anger, as if it all happened yesterday.

She was born into a wealthy family, and when she was just twelve and going on thirteen, rumblings had begun about her marriage.

"For heaven's sake, find her a husband! How long are we going to wait? Else, do we blindfold her and send her to the forest?"—Mother had started her wail already. When she was fourteen, not wanting to wait longer, they had married her off to Parameshwara,—a boy they knew. Parameshwara had no proper job, or even a house for that matter. Her father got him a job as a teacher and she started her life with him in a fifteen-rupee-a-month rented house.

But Nagamma's husband Parameshwara was not the sort who held on to a job. In just four months he had quit the teacher's job. Afterwards, it became a regular practice for him to take up a job under Nagamma's constant nagging and with her father's recommendations—only to give it up on a short notice after getting bored quickly. Later on, he totally gave up the idea of a job. But he put up the appearance of a very busy man with never a minute to spare. He would get out of house in the morning, only to reappear for lunch in the afternoon. And after a lusty siesta, he was off again to return late in the night with no certainty of time.

He had 'work' not only in the town, but out of town too. If Lawyer Shivarama Shetty had to go to Mangalore to appear in the court, he was sure to ask Parameshwara to give him company and the latter would be off with him with no further ado. If someone was going out of town for a *Yakshagana* play, Parameshwara would be too willing to pack his bag and go along.

Parameshwara was overly enthusiastic about attending weddings and other social ceremonies. Nagamma was reluctant, since she did not like to be seen down-to-earth plain at such gatherings while her sisters were in their finest saris and loaded with jewellery. Parameshwara couldn't care less. He was in his elements in such gatherings, becoming loquacious on the local as well as out of town news, national and international affairs and issues; eating to his hearts' content and finally chewing a mouthful of betel leaves at the end most contentedly.

He used to earn some small money as a scribe at the court, of which he gave some to Nagamma for the household expenses. But more often he was likely to talk big about swinging deals, and then lose money, ending up pawning Nagamma's jewellery. At one time he was seized with the idea of setting up a shop,—which he did, only to close it in no time at all, running up large debts in the process.

"Forget it Nagamma, you are much better off now."—said Puranamma. Implied were the five Pandava-like sons of Nagamma.

Indeed, Nagamma was well off now. For all the troubles she had taken, her children had education and were now well settled. They were sending home money and she managed well. But that never prevented her from remembering the bad old days and getting worked up.

"You are right, Puranamma. But what is the point in having things now instead of then,—when I wanted them most?" the words came out faint,—swallowing up her voice.

"The other thing Nagamma, our generation was not bold, if you ask me . . . ." ventured Puranamma.

"Puranamma, What do they know, the present generation girls? They earn some little money and it goes to their head, that is all." Nagamma retorted. "Was it like this in our times? Even to buy poison, we had no money which we could call our own." Nagamma's voice became low. It was not clear what she wanted to say. She had contempt for the modern women who earned; on the other hand, she was bitter that there was no money of her own during her days.

It was the hell-or-high-water-all-that-matters-is-the husband era. What if she was born in a house owning large estate with produce of hundreds of *muras* of rice? Father didn't believe in gifting his daughters. His concern for them was limited to inviting them for festivities in his house. He was very protective about the estate which belonged to the patrilineal, extended family and he was particular that nothing of it should go out. It was no use for her mother to say anything, since the only right she seemed to enjoy was of shedding a few tears for her daughter in difficulty.

The best that could be expected from Parameshwara's pittance of a land in Hattiangadi was about eight or nine *muras* of rice annually. It was just adequate for the family. As for vegetables, Nagamma scrabbled to grow a few vegetables in her backyard,—some of them just above the ranks of weeds,—which were enough for her no-frills cooking. Luckily, there were a few trees in the compound; couple of mango trees, one jackfruit tree and six or seven coconut trees. But two of the coconut trees were barren. Produce of the other trees took care of the family needs with some to spare for sale. During the season of fruits, she would lease out the trees and this small income came in handy for the children's school books. But even in this, Parameshwara was likely to ask for a share and she could not bring herself to say 'No' to that. How could she bear to see her man cadging?

But she couldn't be too docile also,—she had to take care of umpteen things like children's dresses, school fees, books, repairing the roof or the bath,—it was endless,—she had to battle for every little thing. She fought to live and lived to fight,—word for word, countering every argument, and shouting down every insult so much that this combating became her nature. Her real self and sensibilities got crushed under the fifty years of her marriage.

People started saying,—Nagamma is a terrible woman, but that husband of hers is so harmless and guileless! But what was the alternative to being terrible? When Parameshwara's relatively prosperous older brother was building a house and was short of money, he eyed the younger one's piece of land. Parameshwara found no fault in this and was actually willing to sell it to help this brother. Nagamma had stepped in and taken her brother-in-law to task,—"What is it? You would like to see us ruined and out on the streets with our children?" And he had beaten a hasty retreat. Being 'terrible' had saved the day.

Leave alone other people, her own niece, a slip of a girl, was overheard by Nagamma, whispering to someone, "I am really scared of aunt Nagamma. She is horrid. But uncle Parameshwara,—he is so nice. Don't you think so?" Yes my girl! I AM dreadful,—the reason why I could manage my family so far and my children are what they are today. But there was a time when I was like you,—a bright-faced girl playing hop-scotch and talking sweetly. I don't know where she is lost now. The harshness had become so pervasive that the art of talking sweet had been forgotten utterly.

The traits, which were never hers have crept upon her and become her own without her knowledge. Arguments and screaming have made her voice rough and gravely. A scowl on the face, furrowed forehead, simmering anger—they have become a permanent armour. A life that has changed me to a person that is not 'I',—Is it any life at all,—wondered Nagamma.

In the recent past she was becoming angry for no reason and sometimes, more than it was necessary. Actually, as Puranamma said, she was better off now monetarily. But, Parameshwara's nature, in spite of his advancing age, never showed any sign of improvement. Always to himself and to his habits, he never took up even the most minor chores. When she had finished all her household work by afternoon and was dying for a few winks,—he would suddenly start hollering impatiently,—"Coffee, Is my coffee ready?" She now-a-days purposely delayed making coffee to make him wait,—why the unholy hurry anyway!

Though in his seventies, he had not given up his wanderings. Last year, some of the school committee members decided to go to Bombay to raise funds for the school building.

And she was in for a surprise when he declared, packing his bag,—"Look, I am going to Bombay. I believe there is a place for me in Prabhu's car." That is it,—he was off . . . Not a care in the world . . . not bothered about his old wife or the home. That too, when there was a spate of robberies taking place in the town. What to say to this utter casualness?

And then,—what did he do last month . . . ? She was yet to recuperate from an eye surgery when he had run off to Mysore to attend the house warming held by his brother-in-law's granddaughter. His self-centeredness depressed her very much,—'This is how it is going to be till I die,'—she thought.

The streetlights were on and still there was no sign of Anthi. "There is no use waiting for her any longer," she said, getting up, when Puranamma, hearing a voice from a distance, remarked, "Listen, isn't that Anthi's voice?"

Indeed it was, and Anthi materialized shortly, walking briskly towards them with a basket of green grass in her hand and proceeded directly to the cattle-shed saying aloud archly,—"*Arre*! Nagamma is very cross with me!"

Nagamma, who was all set to fire Anthi, broke into a rare smile to say, "Look at this woman's antics!" and then sat again.

"I suppose your son is visiting you." said Puranamma, in a tone suggesting that talks could now continue unhindered. Of course, she had seen him coming in the morning.

"Yes," sighed Nagamma, adding,—"Father and son, each sticks to his own guns. You know that!"

Nagamma's son Narasimha had taken a loan from a bank and constructed a house in Bangalore. Since then he has been after his parents,—"It is enough that you have spent a lifetime in this rented house. Both of you should now come to Bangalore and stay with me."

Parameshwara did not at all like the idea of giving up the town and home, and particularly the town. And Nagamma got all the more irritated by her husband, who acted as if the affairs of that small town were all on his shoulders.

Puranamma was tempted to philosophise,— "Nagamma, isn't this world impermanent? So, what is the purpose of striving for the worldly things like land, home and yard?"

In reality, Parameshwara had got used to a carefree, wandering life and so, mention leaving the town, he would 'chuck, chuck' and say,—"How is that possible, ever?"

"What can one say to a man who says Sun won't rise without him? Say anything more and he is ready with the threat, Go! All of you! I can cook the gruel for myself." said Nagamma with a voice weakened by pain.

Puranamma made a sign to Nagamma to look towards the street and Nagamma turned her head. Madhavi, with her hair up and neatly clipped, a bag hung from her shoulder, and a large suitcase in her hand, was walking past Nagamma's gate. As she passed in front of the gate, she appeared to flash a final, parting smile of recognition. Nagamma was stunned for a moment.

Anthi who had just emerged from the cattle-shed and saw this, grumbled, "My work has all gone haywire watching the big fight at that Madhavi's house." as she took the milk pot into the house. And then coming out, she commented, "Sun is already down. Can't tarry a minute. I am off." Dusting off her sari she walked out of the gate.

It was time to light the lamps and Puranamma also got up. Nagamma walked home as if she was in a daze. As she lighted the oil-wick in front of the deity's idol and was reciting the verse, "*Dipum jyoti parabrahmam . . . .*", the image of Madhavi walking down the road with the suitcase leapt to her mind and, suddenly, she felt the worry-lines in her face smoothen up. She too had packed up not once, but three times in her long life. But then she had nowhere to go. Every time it so happened that she would fill up the suitcase with her saris, also with a few tear-drops which sank in, and later, as can be expected, she would quietly unpack without much ado.

She knelt and bowed to the shrine and remained thus for a longish time. What could be the real nature of this Nagamma? She groped within herself for an identity.

The next day morning, when Narasimha was going to buy the bus-ticket, Nagamma surprised everybody by asking him to buy a ticket for her too. "If your father wants to stay, let him! He can stick to the town and the house for his dear life." she said. It was as easy as turning a page.

Though quite unexpected, Parameshwara didn't show it. He just said gruffly,—"Do as you like." under the mistaken impression that it was only a bluff.

After two days, when Nagamma was really walking out of the gate with a bag in her hand, Puranamma was seen rushing to her. She applied vermilion to her forehead and also gave her two packets of it.

As Narasimha walked in front with the 'hold-all' and the suitcase, Parameshwara followed, holding up the end of his dhoti in the left hand, swinging his right arm and talking loudly to his son.

Seated inside the bus, Nagamma could overhear her husband below telling an acquaintance nonchalantly,—"I told her to spend a few days at her son's place, she gets bored, after all, you know! When Narasimha asked her to go with him, I said,—let her go. But me? Forget it! Will I find time for such visits?"

When Nagamma, sitting back with a sense of relief, saw her husband talking and gesticulating spiritedly, she did not know whether to cry or laugh.

It is six or seven years since then and Nagamma has not shown her face here, not even once. And now, whenever Puranamma sees the gate across the street and the platform attached to it, she remembers her friend wistfully and the old friendship and intimate talks come back to her. And she asks herself in despair,—"*Ayyo!* Have those days really gone forever?"

THE DAUGHTER
COMES HOME

The palanquin was rocking agreeably. From time to time, Laxmi drew the curtain aside to peep out and get her bearings so that she could estimate the distance left to reach Chakrapur. And every time she did so, Aithala who was walking briskly behind the palanquin with a wet cloth-cover over his head to protect his head against the merciless sun beating down, ran up to her to ask solicitously.

'Well, madam, are you tired?' or 'Madam, would you care for a coconut drink?'

Aithala was the 'family priest' for the Kemmady house of Laxmi's husband and, before him, his grandfather too had been their priest. Such had been this priestly connection that Aithala was considered a part of their household. This explained the ease with which Laxmi's mother-in-law, Seethamma, could put him on to this errand.

'Say, Aithala-re,' she had said to the elderly man, 'won't you please go with Laxmi and see her to her father's house?' Aithala had agreed without a murmur, as he always did to any errand that the Kemmady house threw up for him.

It was only on the previous day that the news had reached them through a messenger from Chakrapur, that Laxmi's father had taken ill. The message had also said that Laxmi should be sent to Chakrapur immediately. It was clear from the look on her mother-in-law's face that it had got her deeply worried. She had reason to worry more because Laxmi's husband, Narasa, was away from home to attend a meeting of the landowners called by the British imperial Government in the distant town of Coimbatore, a good four days journey from the village.

Though Laxmi did not know what exactly the message said, she had been feeling very uneasy while churning the cream early in the morning. Apart from the bad dreams the night before, there was now this bad omen of her right eyelid quivering involuntarily, and this unsettled her mind. As she turned the rope back and forth and the foamy cream swirled around in the churn, her thoughts wandered off, bringing a lump to her throat and tears to her eyes.

Seethamma did not have any daughters and as such, was excessively fond of her daughter-in-law. So much so that it precluded any thought in her mind for the affection that Laxmi's parents would have for her. She was so possessive about her young daughter-in-law that she rarely allowed her to visit her parents in Chakrapur.

Wiping off her tears, Laxmi started collecting the butter. Finishing with one churn, she started off on another one brimming with buffalo milk, the urns almost coming up to her chest. If she started churning at dawn, the chore would get over only when the day broke. It was a chore dear to her, and that was the reason why she preferred to do it herself, in spite of the house having a large retinue of servants. She had taken upon herself the full responsibility of making butter oil and storing it properly. If one jar of butter-oil from cow's milk was meant for the house deity, another from the buffalo's milk was for the ordinary mortals. And never the twain was to come in contact as per the rigid rules of the Kemmady house.

As she was coming into the house after washing the churn and the churning-rod at the well, she had heard her mother-in-law calling to the children, trying to wake them up. Then she said to her daughter-in-law, 'Laxmi, I don't think you should take the children along, except of course, the little one.' The firm implication that she was after all being sent to her father's house greatly relieved Laxmi, and this had quickened her steps as she hastened into the house.

The blaze of the sun was intensifying as they progressed. Little Shankari, who had gone to sleep on the shoulder of Devappa, the servant, woke up and started crying. Laxmi took the baby from Devappa for breast-feeding. And as the baby's eyes drooped again, she remembered something, and leaning out, called out to Aithala, 'I say, could you arrange for a few tender coconuts? I would like to carry them for my father.'

Aithala was silent for a moment. Meanwhile, she continued, 'You know father loves coconut water.' She craned her neck out of the palanquin and scanned the treetops for nuts. Thought Aithala bitterly, 'The young lady should understand. How can I tell her? It breaks my heart.' But looking at her face he softened and called out to a servant, 'Hey, Giriya, go pluck a few good ones.' Then he too went along to choose the best tree and the nuts.

Handing over the sleeping child back to Devappa, Laxmi got down from the palanquin. She drank from the tender coconut that Giriya had chopped for her. It tasted divine in the oppressive heat of the noon. She felt vastly refreshed.

Suddenly, when the reality dawned on her that she was now actually going to Chakrapur, she felt a burst of happiness within her, and getting back into the palanquin she was in a very happy frame of mind.

It must have been seventeen years since she had got married at the age of seven and gone to her husband's house. But the number of visits she had made to her mother's place could be counted on the fingers. In the year she got married her mother-in-law herself had given in to Laxmi's tears and taken her to Chakrapur. But then, she too had stayed on there, clearly indicating that she intended to take back Laxmi with her. It was probably after another three years that the girl managed to go and visit her parents again. Even at the time of her first confinement, instead of going to her mother's place as was the custom, it was her mother who had had to come to Kemmady house for the delivery. Though Laxmi did go with the new-born to Chakrapur, it must have been just for a week.

In fact, none of her visits to Chakrapur lasted for more than ten days. Sometimes, the visit would be planned for a longer period, but suddenly, unannounced, either a palanquin or a bullock cart would turn up from Kemmadi to fetch her back. Whenever Laxmi's father came to visit her, he would invariably propose to take her with him for a few days, but each and every time, her mother-in-law came up with some seemingly strong reason to put her visits off. It would either be a festival or the harvest season or again it could be somebody's illness—her own included.

Ironically, Laxmi's problem was an excessively affectionate mother-in-law instead of the traditional spiteful one. Her mother-in-law loved to keep her in sight all the time. When Laxmi had come to Kemmady house as a seven-year-old bride, she had not even known how to drape a sari around herself. Seethamma used to do that for her every day. Having only a son, her daughter-in-law was very dear to her,—the apple of her eye, so to say.

Laxmi had grown up since those days, both physically and mentally. She would not now speak her mind even when the memories of Chakrapur stirred her intensely. That is why, her father, Keshava Bhatta, who knew her nature well, would often visit her on his own and stay with her for a couple of days. Once in a while, he would bring his wife Parvati along with him on such visits. He thought this was the price he had to pay for giving his daughter to a family of high status.

Keshava Bhatta was a Brahmin priest at the Chakrapur temple and, though of modest means, was a well-known personality in his area. Since he used to preside over the performance of the religious rites in the local temple on behalf of the Maharaja of Mysore, he was even known as the 'royal priest'. Reputed though he was the marriage alliance for his daughter from the Kemmady house, with its unmatched wealth and power in the whole area, had come as a total surprise.

After the death of her husband, Seethamma herself had to take over the management of the Kemmady house. It was no mean task to manage the vast estate at the age of only twenty-three and at the same time take care of her four-year old son. But she was a woman of great resolve and she succeeded in this task to everyone's admiration.

It was at the annual festival of the Chakrapur temple that Seethamma first saw Laxmi, who was then 'Meenakshi' to her parents. Sitting in the balcony of the temple meant exclusively for the Kemmady house, Seethamma was watching the festivities when her eyes fell on Meenakshi, who was sitting below among the girls of her age. Seethamma was struck by the radiance of her young face. She decided on the spot that this would be the wife for her son, Narasa.

Laxmi was then not even seven years old. The pretty little girl was draped in a sari and her hair was neatly plaited, adorned with strings of jasmine and *abbalige* flowers. She was watching the ceremonies with her big, bright eyes unaware that she was being observed. Seethamma lost no time in making enquiries about this sunny little girl and even managed to get near the girl and talk to her.

To Keshava Bhatta, it happened as if in a dream—his being called to the Kemmady house for talks regarding the marriage and the engagement taking place immediately thereafter. According to the wishes of Seethamma and contrary to the custom, the wedding ceremonies were held in the Kemmady house itself.

At the age of seven, Laxmi was hardly three feet tall. But the twenty-year-old bridegroom, Narasa, was as tall 'as a palm tree'. At the time of marriage, during the ceremony of exchanging garlands, the little bride had to be held high by her father so that her hands could reach up to garland the bridegroom.

When the wedding festivities were finally over and Seethamma said that the bride would remain in Kemmady house, her parents were taken aback. They had thought that their little girl would continue to stay with them till she would come of age, as was the custom. But Seethamma was firm. She said that the bride was now not only her daughter-in-law, but also her daughter and it was totally her responsibility to bring up the child. Keshava Bhatta had to bow to her wishes. To let go of the only daughter was very painful to the parents.

Meenakshi was the last and the only child to survive among the ten children born to them. After burying the nine children one after the other, they had lost all hopes of ever having a child. Whenever he found his wife Parvati grieving over the lost children, Keshava Bhatta would console her. "Don't grieve, Paru. When it is not the will of the Chakrapur-goddess, is there anything for us to say? It is our fate, after all."

But when the Chakrapur goddess did bless them with one more child,—a baby girl, they were determined to break the spell and save the child by any means. For this, they had to resort to an unusual subterfuge. The baby, as soon as it was born, was taken out through the backyard to the foot of the hill behind the house, where it was placed inside a freshly dug pit in the ground, symbolizing a grave. They even threw a pinch of soil on it and returned home, thus tricking the Fate into believing that the child had died. Then their servant Sesi, quietly went to the pit, picked up the child and filled up the pit after dropping a live chicken into it. She brought the child to Parvati and 'sold' it to her for two measures of rice and a coconut. With this elaborate charade, Fate was thoroughly fooled and Laxmi, nee Meenakshi survived.

When the palanquin bearers had gone away to drink water, Aithala said to Laxmi, 'Not much distance left now, may be about half-an-hour's journey. Look! You can even see the spire of the Chakrapur temple from here.'

Laxmi became thoughtful. Would her father be at the temple now? How could he be there if he was ill? She could not recollect a time when her father had actually been bed-ridden. He had always been healthy and strong. He used to boast that he could eat and digest even stones.

Even if he was unwell, it never bothered him, and he was not the sort to lie down in bed because of illness. Once, during the nine-day festival of 'Navaratri', though he was running high fever, he had continued to bathe in cold water, worship the idol and conduct the temple celebrations with all the usual pomp and without missing a single step of the ritual.

Unknown fears gnawed at her heart as she thought of her father lying in bed—so unlike of him. But on earlier visits, how joyous she used to become as she neared home! She sighed when it occurred to her that it was more than five or six years since she had come here last.

She was aware that the day she was to arrive, her parents would run about the house in great excitement. Father would perform the temple rituals quickly to return home earlier than usual.

'Look, Paru, our little daughter has come,' he would call out to his wife from outside; and when she rushed out of the house leaving the chores half-done, poor mother would find that she had been fooled. He would fool her mother several times before Laxmi actually arrived and, by then, her mother was bound to disbelieve him. So, when Laxmi really arrived, her mother would refuse to come out till she was right at the doorstep and called out to her. She would then complain to Laxmi about her father, giving an exaggerated account of his petty perfidies which Laxmi would find very amusing. Her father's quirky sense of humour and propensity for practical jokes resulted in laughter bubbling and spreading all around him.

Then there was this matter of his love for food. He was a big eater and his appetite for food was as extreme as his sense of humour. Her mother liked to surprise him sometimes by making his favourite snack of *doses*, thick and spongy, that she would pile high on a plate, cover it, and keep it behind the stove. She would then go out as usual to have a chat with the neighbours or to the temple. Once it so happened that father came home early that day and went to search the kitchen as was his habit and found the pile of '*doses*' hid behind the stove and made a short work of it. Afterwards, he kept the plate covered as before and quietly walked out.

When mother came home and found him engrossed in his work in the outer veranda, she sought to surprise him by grandly announcing that his favourite '*dose*' was waiting for him.

Father dramatically perked up and said eagerly, 'Oh! Really, bring on the '*dose*'. I am famished and the drums of hunger are beating in my stomach' and followed her to the kitchen. But mother was in for a shock when she lifted the lid and found an empty plate, whereupon father started howling that he had been tricked and made a fool of. The whole thing left his poor wife utterly embarrassed and confused, till of course, she found out the trick he had played on her. Laxmi chuckled softly remembering many such mischiefs her father had played.

The blaze of the sun and the gentle rocking of the palanquin made Laxmi drowsy and, in this state of half-consciousness, many thoughts passed through her mind. Suddenly she became suspicious of this whole affair of her father's illness. Something told her that this reported illness was not really true. There was good reason for doubting it.

When he had visited her a few months back, he was talking to her alone and one thing led to another and he had told her in a conspiratorial tone, 'Meenakshi, don't you worry! Let the monsoon be over. Your mother-in-law has agreed to send you home after the rains. I have a nice plan if she goes back on her words. I'll send an urgent message to her—'I'm seriously ill. Please send my daughter immediately'—and he had laughed heartily with a hand over his mouth.

The memory of this incident brought her cheer. Conscious that she was now nearing home, she got the feeling that there was some magic in the very air of Chakrapur. There was a world of difference between the solemn atmosphere of the Kemmady house and the easy-going ways of her parents' house. Hardly anyone laughed or talked aloud in her husband's house. But here, her parents' house was filled with the loud laughter and the booming banter of her father or the high-pitched retorts of her mother. Though there were only two of them, the racket in the house appeared enough to blow the roof off!

Sometimes, when father was in high spirits, he would start singing songs from the folk opera 'Yakshagana'—and the neighbours would gather around him. His deep voice, superb commentaries and the sheer style of his delivery sent the listeners into raptures. As he got into the spirit of things, he would even get up and start jigging in the 'Yakshagana' style.

When she spotted the house from afar, somehow the atmosphere did not look normal to her. There was no sign of her father, holding up the edge of his *dhoti* and running up to meet her; and no sign of her mother either hurrying down from the upper veranda to the lower one and then to the yard, wiping her hands dry with the end of her sari and rushing to meet her.

If the atmosphere about the house looked depressing, there was a strong reason for it.

Keshava Bhatta was lying down in his room by the side of the veranda, covered from head to toe in a thick blanket. Parvati, in the kitchen, closed her eyes and said, 'Oh God!' when she spotted Aithala through the kitchen window. Her legs trembled. 'Oh! Goddess of Chakrapur! Help me in this trial. It will be a disaster if I stumble. Give me strength to face the situation, Oh! Mother Goddess!' With such fervent prayers on her lips, she came out to meet them.

When she faced her daughter in the veranda, her eyes were filled with tears. Laxmi broke down upon seeing her mother's distress.

After washing his hands and feet at the well, Aithala went straight to Keshava Bhatta with a dour demeanour.

Her mother stopped Laxmi from following him. Taking her aside towards the kitchen, she tried to prepare her daughter for what was to follow so as not to upset her father. It had the desired effect on Laxmi as she could collect herself before she entered her father's room.

Keshava Bhatta's condition looked pathetic. Though it was summer time and the room hot and stifling, he was shivering under the thick blankets. As if that was not enough, Aithala, after coming in, had closed the window at the head of the bed, saying that air current was not good for the patient.

After solemnly hearing about the nature and intensity of the fever in great detail, Aithala tried to give them courage by repeatedly saying, "There is really no reason to panic"—even as he feared the worst. He was very solicitous, instructing them about the proper care of the patient and the correct course of treatment. A number of medications involving grinding, pounding, boiling and such processes, as also the various stages of their preparations were prescribed by Aithala.

Parvati heard him patiently and said, 'In fact, he is somewhat better today. A couple of days ago, he was lying unconscious.' Then seeing her husband's vacant stare, she said, 'Yesterday we had virtually lost all hopes . . .' So saying she covered her face with the end of her sari to hide her grief.

Keshava Bhatta was in no condition to join the conversation. All he could do was to roll his eyes or move his hands weakly. One or two words did escape from his lips, but Laxmi could not recognize the trembling voice as that of her father. No longer able to stand the depressing atmosphere of the room, she went out.

When it was time for lunch, a lad from the neighbourhood, Anantha, came to help. He brought a few banana leaves from a plant in the backyard and spread them on the floor in a line for serving lunch. By the time he began to serve, starting with salt and pickles, Aithala, who had finished a quick bath at the well, came in for lunch.

Bhatta's nephew, Surya, who arrived there after finishing the worship at the temple, also joined them for lunch. The atmosphere was sombre as the lunch progressed silently.

After taking a short nap while the palanquin bearers were served their meals, Aithala made preparations for his departure. He went to Keshava Bhatta to bid him good-bye, but when he saw him asleep, he did not feel like disturbing the sick man. As he went out quietly, his eyes were moist as a groan escaped from him involuntarily—'Oh, Great Lord!' Taking leave of the others and uttering words of reassurance, Aithala started for Kemmady.

No sooner had Aithala crossed the gate, there was a flurry of activities in Bhatta's room. The shutters of the windows were flung wide open with a bang. Laxmi rushed into the room with her baby in her arms and saw her father, who had been lying still in the bed like a log, flinging the blankets away and getting up from his bed with great alacrity.

Wiping his perspiring body with a towel, he winked at Laxmi and asked, "How was my performance?" He continued with a mischievous twinkle in his eyes, "It was so easy fooling your Aithala . . . . And it was great fun listening to him holding forth about medicines and the treatments!"

He grabbed the baby from Laxmi's arms and, holding his grandchild in his arms, started doing a '*yakshagana*' jig before breaking into an impromptu song about a daughter coming home.

He was not short of an audience, what with Anantha, Surya, Laxmi and mother all gathered around him, cheering him loudly. Now, this was how Laxmi had always remembered her parents' house.

Laxmi's joy knew no bounds and her laughter would not cease—and she had a lot of catching up to do.

THERE WAS A MESSAGE

There was a time when Jalaja-*Chikki*—a somewhat distant but a very affectionate aunt—meant everything to Narmada. But Narmada was then a mere child, and isn't it true of all children that they let their love flow freely towards anyone who loves and indulges in them? It is only as children grow older and are influenced by opinions, injunctions and whispered secrets from others that their love becomes increasingly constrained, conditional and subjective. So it was with Narmada; with a kind of indifference for Jalaja having crept into her, she had kept away from the latter for a long time. But now, after many years, she was on her way to Jalaja's place once again, carrying the weight of Appanna-*Chikkappa*'s message, and unsure of the feelings that surged within her.

Aunt Jalaja's house was known as 'The House of Pillars', and it was just fifteen-minute walk from

Narmada's house. But if one took the shortcut and ran all the way, like Narmada did when she was young, it could be reached in barely five minutes. As a child, Narmada would often dash to *Chikki*'s house, either after school or on holidays, drawn by the great attraction it held for her. And there was no knowing when she would return home—it could be after two hours, or even two days. This was true not only of her and her sister but of all the children in their family. In fact, Nagu, her cousin, once stayed there for so many days that his mother had to come, cane in hand, to take him home.

Just two persons lived in the old, sprawling, 'House of Pillars'—Jalaja and Appanna. Both of them adored children, and the children, in turn were drawn to them like iron filings to a magnet.

'The House of Pillars' had an impressive front porch with a row of robust teak pillars—from which apparently the house took its name—supporting its wooden ceiling. Next to the porch was a large hall with an inner courtyard and from there onwards the house spread aimlessly, encompassing kitchen, dining hall, and many chambers. Behind the house was a large pond and a clump of trees, beyond which were paddy fields and a picturesque river with coconut trees lining its bank.

Narmada remembered the time she had enthusiastically agreed to get into the pond with Jalaja, in a bid to learn swimming. With two 'hollow' coconuts tied around her waist to give her confidence, if not buoyancy, she had just waded into ankle deep water, when she started screaming, 'Ayyo *Chikki*, please! I don't want to learn swimming or anything!', and tried to scramble back to the shore. Pushing her back into the water, Jalaja-*Chikki* had exhorted, 'Nothing to be frightened of . . . come on! Just keep flapping your arms and legs in the water.'—That was Jalaja-*Chikki*.

Children just couldn't resist Jalaja, who readily danced to their tune. Regardless of the number of guests she had in the house, she would finish her chores quickly to get ready to arrange programmes to entertain the children. Announcing exciting plans for the kids such as, 'Let's go to the river front' or 'we'll have picnic in the woods' or, 'I'll talk to the boatman . . . . we'll go boating!' she would keep them in a state of constant excitement.

Chikkappa was no less. Jalaja used to say that he became ten years younger when he was with the children. If he had to go to the grove to get the coconuts picked or oversee the servicing of the water pump in the paddy field, he wouldn't fail to pick a child from among those who happened to be in the house at that moment and take the little one along, holding its hand or seating it on his head or shoulder.

Having made the children excited about learning to swim, Jalaja Chikki had got them ready before day break and marched them to the pond.

Chikkappa, hovering around the pond asked *Chikki* teasingly, 'Jalaja, you want me to teach you how to swim?' and she had glowered at him in mock anger and chased him off.

Tying a pair of hollow coconuts to each child, she got them all into the water. Appanna by then had slipped in to join them, and with him in the water, the fun began. It started with Appanna scooping water in both hands to splash it on Jalaja. Soon, everyone joined in, and the whole pond erupted with water splashing all around; squeals of laughter and screams of delight filled the air. Two groups of children formed spontaneously and they splashed water at each other ferociously, as if it was some sport.

Jalaja's stern rebuke to Appanna, 'It is always you who starts the mischief!' fell on deaf ears.

Narmada was delirious with delight, and later had wondered why elders disapproved of the very people whom children loved.

Seemingly everyone made disparaging remarks about Jalaja-*Chikki* behind her back.

Narmada's eldest aunt or '*Doddathe*' couldn't stand the sight of Jalaja. 'What a woman! She doesn't have the slightest notion of shame or honour,' she railed, sitting on the ledge of the upper porch, with one leg tucked under her haunch while massaging the other one with her hand, as was her wont.

'Why did she have to turn up at the last minute at Raghu's *upanayana*? Would anyone have missed her?'

Doddathe's sister, Rukmini, who was engaged in sorting the spinach bundles spread before her, rolled her eyes for good effect while giving an explanation sarcastically, 'It seems Raghu had threatened—Jalaja*the*! If you don't turn up, I just won't go through the ceremony.'

'Oh . . . yeah? Did they welcome her with a garland?' asked *Doddathe* tartly, matching her sister's sarcasm.

It was difficult to understand such contempt for Jalaja considering her endearing qualities. With a slim figure and attractive looks, Jalaja compelled lingering attention. Her talk seemed to sparkle with her silvery voice. She had good memory for people and was concerned about their likes and dislikes.

When Seenu was visiting her after years, she remembered, despite the flurry, that he was allergic to eggplants, and said while serving him the meal, 'Seenu, I know eggplant doesn't agree with you. So I have made gourd-curry especially for you.'

Jalaja was equally solicitous to guests even while not being the hostess,—like at a wedding where she herself would be a guest. Even during the bustle of such an event, remembering that Gujjadi-*Ajja* suffered from acidity, she had offered him some milk before the meal.

When coffee was served after a meal, Jalaja had reminded her sister Laxmi, 'Brother-in-law prefers tea, doesn't he?' and despite Lakshmi's nonchalant response—He won't die if he took coffee once in a while—she had gone ahead and got the tea specially made for him, and herself brought it to him. And if she were at a familiar house, she would have rushed in and made the tea herself.

Women who disliked her, said snidely, 'Thank god, I don't have such urge to please people', or dismissively, 'Oh, all this soft-soaping! We can't stand it!'

As a matter of fact, the elderly women who found fault with Jalaja were ever ready to accept her help without any reservation when it came to their own need. Even while mumbling—We are incapable of such fawning, only Jalaja can do that—they would gladly let Jalaja attend to them. Like letting her get them water in a jug to wash their hand after a community meal if she offered to do so, saying—You needn't go all the way to the well; it is so slippery. I'll get some water for you to wash your hand right here at this plantain tree.

When someone wanted to go to the distant Anegudde temple to make an offering or for a festival there, and couldn't find anyone who would accompany them, Jalaja had volunteered, '*Akka*, if you like, I can take you there. Let me see . . . eighth is Monday, ninth Tuesday . . . . Let's go on Wednesday. If we leave early in the morning, we can return by sunset.'

Jalaja's jackfruit *happala*, her *ragi-sandige* and her mango pickles were in great demand. And when *Doddathe*, who seethed at the very mention of Jalaja's name, had asked her, 'Jalaja, have you made any *ragi-sandige* this season? Can't do a thing these days what with this cursed arthritis that has crippled me . . . 'Jalaja had taken the hint with alacrity. With words of sympathy like—'Poor *Doddakka* is in bad shape'—Jalaja had happily packed some *happala* in a plastic bag for her.

Chikkappa kept himself insulated from all squabbles and backbiting. A man of great equanimity, he confined himself to his work. But if engaged in conversation, he could be so engrossing that one wouldn't realize how the time went. As he sat cross-legged, chewing betel and talked—no topic would be missed—whether be religious myths, philosophy or politics.

Of medium height, he normally wore dhoti and a close collared *jubba* when going out; a shawl would be added for special occasions like a marriage or a festival. But at home it was *dhoti* and a long shirt with short sleeves.

When Narmada remembered the rapid changes that took place in the relationship with her relatives in the House of Pillars, the incident that came to her memory instantly was something that fell on her ears when *Doddathe*, that is, her elder aunt, was talking to her mother and was saying, 'She has ensnared poor Appanna . . . . And I dare say, sold our family honour for a copper coin! You are stupid, Rama. Listen to me. Don't let your daughters go there. I don't approve of it. Imagine what people who saw them going there would make of it.'

That was it! Restrictions were increasingly placed on the children visiting Jalaja-*Chikki*'s house, who till then had flocked to her house as and when they wished. The grown-ups retained some contact with Jalaja to the extent needed, but children were curtly told to keep off! Any excitement at the prospects of going to *Chikki* would be firmly curbed by the elders' anger—an anger that seemed to lack any reason.

Once when Jalaja had come to visit Narmada's mother, Narmada had scrambled down the stairs from upstairs upon hearing her voice but was severely reprimanded by her mother, 'What's the matter, Busybody! Where to? And who sent for you? Go grind the rice in the grinder.' And that rebuke had ended with a resounding blow on her back. The only reason for poor Jalaja's visit had been to offer some help. She had come to ask Narmada's mother if she needed black-gram to be ground, and that she could get it done if wanted.

It was not clear if Jalaja-*Chikki* was unaware of the goings on behind her back or she didn't take it seriously despite knowing about it. Anyway Jalaja was always the same. She seemed unaffected even as others increasingly hardened their attitude towards her. When her sister-in-law, Rukmini, who used to be outright rude to her, fell ill and Appanna brought his sister home, it was Jalaja who looked after her for months together.

What really touched Narmada, even amazed her was that Jalaja-*Chikki*, in spite of all the mud-slinging, never quarrelled with or even talked harshly to anyone.

Searching the memories of the time she had spent at Jalaja's house during her childhood, Narmada had realized that latters' love for Appanna-*Chikkappa* was intense and immeasurable and that an integral part of the fun children had in the House of Pillars those days was the close companionship between Jalaja—*Chikki* and Appanna-*Chikkappa*. And she vividly remembered how it was.

If *Chikkappa* said, 'Look, I have to catch the first bus to Mangalore tomorrow morning', Jalaja-*Chikki* would get up at four in the morning to light the hearth under the bathroom-cauldron to make hot water for his bath, and then a full-fledged breakfast would be readied by her even if he protested saying, 'Jalaja, you are impossible! I had told you that coffee was all that I wanted.' She would brush aside his protest with, 'You know how bad it is to drink coffee on an empty stomach? It was no big deal making it anyway.'

Jalaja made life easy for *Chikkappa* in every possible way: keeping warm water handy when he returned home, making all the arrangements for him to worship at the house-shrine immediately after his bath in the mornings, preparing the customary *paan* for him to chew promptly after his meal.

Jalaja was so adept at gauging him that she knew if he had headache by his expression or joked, 'Looks like a fellow here wants coffee' by the way he approached her in the kitchen.

Appanna too cared as much for Jalaja. He hankered for her companionship, calling out to her with the seemingly constant refrain of 'Jalaja . . . Jalajakshi'—to say something to her or to consult her, and sometimes even to tease her when he got an opportunity. At times he pretended to suffer from backache to garner her sympathy that came in the form of soothing words or if he was lucky, by way of more soothing massage of his back.

Sitting on the swing in the porch and chewing *paan,* he wouldn't give up coaxing her till she too joined him on the swing and took a *paan* from his hand to chew. He was used to consulting her on all issues big and small—like asking her 'What do you say to planting some twenty more coconut plants this year, Jalaja?', or—'Should I tell Venkatesh to bring his lorry next week to pick up the nuts?'

They had their disagreements, of course. But then their arguments were amusing to the kids. When *Chikki* was all excited with the children being with her and was busy making arrangements for them to sleep for the night, *Chikkappa*, eyeing Jalaja with a long face and pretending to be unhappy, had said aloud, 'Nobody cares for me anymore, . . . Looks like Jalaja might throw me out for the night. May be, I have to sleep outside.'

'My God, what a melodrama!' she said in exasperation, 'What have these poor children done to you? Look, you can have your share—you manage the boys . . . . All of you sleep upstairs; the girls will be with me here.'

When *Chikkappa* invaded the kitchen, ostensibly to help *Chikki*, and she wanting him out, the whole thing became uproariously funny with the kids too joining in the shouting and jostling.

Watching the relation between the two that was so much fun, Narmada had often wondered why her patents too couldn't be like them.

Narmada's feelings toward Jalaja-*Chikki* may have begun to change the day she was playing '*gajiga*' with Latthi in the porch of Putta*the*'s house. She had overheard Putta*the* talking agitatedly to her mother inside the house.

'When I see the unholy things going in that house, which was after all once my sister's, it is like a knife being turned in my stomach. Kamakshi—bless her soul!—is no more, but has been spared this terrible indignity . . . . My father had told Appanna to remarry—so that the child would be looked after well. But did he listen? And what is going on now—is it pretty? At least, shouldn't that widow have some sense in her?'

At this, Narmada, tossing the small marble-sized *gajiga*-nut up, had raised her eyebrows questioningly at Latthi.

'Don't you know?' whispered Latthi. 'It seems Jalaja-*Chikki* and Appanna-*Chikkappa* went to a movie together yesterday.'

'So?'

'So . . . it shows how dumb you are!' Latthi said in irritation, tapping Narmada's forehead with her *gajiga*.

'Are they husband and wife that they can go to movie together?' she asked rhetorically.

Continuing the game nonchalantly, she took her turn to toss up the gajiga and then picked up those on the floor quickly before catching the one in the air as it came down.

It was Latthi again who later explained to a bewildered Narmada all the subtleties of man-woman relationships, putting on the superior air of an elder sister. Narmada, listened to the story of the house she had played in since her childhood as if the house was new to her, and became quite disturbed by what she heard. The relationship that had given her innocent mind so much of cheer suddenly began to look ugly.

'I'd never have believed that Jalaja-*Chikki* was such a wicked woman,' said Narmada, hardening her heart to the extent she could bring herself to say such a thing.

'I didn't either. But I stopped going there as soon as I got wind of it. You also don't go there, Nammu,' advised Latthi, as if she wasn't four but forty years older than Narmada.

Then, what about Jalaja-*Chikki*'s love, affection and good qualities? Were they all pretences? Why didn't she meet a sudden death, like all those evil women did in the movies? My God, what a hypocrite!—In the wake of the surging anger and rage, Narmada felt a stab of pain.

Seized by a sudden doubt, she questioned Latthi, 'If what you say is true, What about the mark on her forehead?'

'Oh, that! That's only a tattoo!'

Narmada then remembered it—a grain sized tattoo exactly between the eyebrows of that attractive round face, and she also remembered the incident during Pammi's wedding-

Sheela was in charge of welcoming the guests, and she had assigned Narmada the job of offering *kum-kum* to female guests who were *sumangalis*,—married but not widowed. And Sheela herself began to handing flowers to the *sumangalis* for wearing in their hair.

As she went about her assignment, Narmada offered *kum-kum* to Jalaja, bypassing the elderly *sumangalis* who really mattered. It didn't strike Narmada that Chikki, being a widow, was not eligible to wear *kum-kum*, and that *sumangalis*—old or young—would resent a widow being treated as equal to them. As soon as Sheela noticed this serious lapse of etiquette, she came running, and snatched the *kum-kum*-case from Narmada, and handing her a fan, told her to fan the guests instead. Narmada was left confused, not yet being familiar with the treacherous rules of social mores, and probably having the notion that all women who looked good or young were *sumangalis.*

Latthi let her on it or Narmada came to know about it on her own as she grew up—either way—she gradually became aware of other aspects of the lives of those who inhabited the House of Pillars. She came to learn that *Chikkappa* had been married at a young age to Kamakshi, that is, Puttathe's older sister but his wife died during childbirth, leaving behind the new born child—Keshava. Appanna was only twenty-six years old when he became a widower, but never bothered to remarry, defying advices and counsels from the people around him. His mother, Seshamma, was so worried by his refusal to remarry that—it was said—it caused her to become bed-ridden.

The House of Pillars had been divided earlier, during the lifetime of Appanna's father, Sadashiva, between himself and his younger brother. When Appanna was widowed, he was living in one wing with his child Keshava, while his cousin Venkappa lived in the other with his wife Jalaja and their children. By this time, with the sisters and later the daughters too, getting married and the brothers and sons going away in search of jobs, both the wings of the house, once bustling with people, had already begun to look empty.

Appanna was the younger of two brothers and his elder brother had already settled in Bangalore. So, it was just Appanna with his young son Keshava and his mother Seshamma in the eastern wing of the house, while in the western wing it was his cousin Venkappa and his wife Jalaja.

Jalaja, with the encouragement of her husband, helped Appanna in looking after both his young son as well as his old, ailing mother.

Appanna and his cousin had married around the same time. While Appanna was widowed early on, the tragedy visited the other wing just after three years when Venkappa died suddenly, leaving Jalaja all alone in the western wing of the house.

For Jalaja, the refuge of her parents' house was not an option after her widowhood since she had lost both her parents when she was a child. Although she had four brothers, they were bitterly divided among themselves and she did not want to seek a place amidst these feuding siblings. So, she decided to stay put in the house which was hers by right, while continuing to look after Appanna's young son, Keshava, for whom she had taken great liking, as well as his mother Seshamma, by making frequent visits to the eastern wing as before.

Seshamma used to tell Jalaja in great sorrow about the decline of the once-thriving House of Pillars, blaming it all on 'the evil eye that has been cast'. She recalled evocatively of a house that once was lively and bustling with family members, where guests thronged and were served meals in rows that filled the main hall.

As Jalaja sat listening to this account of the past glory of the family and lamentations about its end, she felt intense sympathy for her old relation. But she realised that it was a sorrow that wouldn't subside howsoever being consoled.

Sharing her pain and sorrow with Jalaja, consoling herself and being consoled by her, Seshamma finally breathed her last. But before her death, the walls between the two wings of the house had lost its relevance. Seshamma had seen to it that there was just one kitchen now in place of the two which existed before. And this arrangement happened to be convenient for the widower, Appanna. It spared him the bother of managing the household.

When Keshava grew up, he went to live with Appanna's brother in the city of Bangalore for his schooling. After finishing his studies, he found a job there and his bonds with the hometown became weak. Though he occasionally visited his father, he would stay just for a day, or at the most two, in his parent's house. Thus it was only Appanna and Jalaja who lived in that large house; and on its own, an unusual relationship developed between the two.

After the 'enlightening' conversation with Latthi, Narmada did not step into Jalaja-*Chikki*'s house again. Even if she met her by chance, she felt kind of awkward and resentful while talking to her face to face.

Narmada had settled down in Bangalore after her marriage. Though she came home to her parents at least once a year, she found no occasion to visit Jalaja-*Chikki*. Of course, an opportunity presents itself only when one desires it. She had recently been to Keshava's house in

Bangalore, where she had seen an ailing *Chikkappa*, lying alone in bed in a well-furnished room and staring blankly at the ceiling. And this had made her decide, while on her way to her parents' house in the hometown that she would definitely meet Jalaja-*Chikki* this time.

When Appanna had fallen ill and became bedridden, Keshava had taken him to his house in Bangalore as otherwise it would have been difficult for him to visit his hometown frequently to check his father's condition. Besides, he did not want people to accuse him of neglecting his ailing father despite being well-placed.

Pramila, Keshava's wife, had said to Narmada, 'He must be past seventy, right? Still, he doesn't have an iota of shame. Two days ago . . . would you believe it . . . he wanted to know if Jalaja could be brought here! The old man is senile . . . . I said,—nothing doing! Then he says—it doesn't suit me here; shall I go back home? Just see . . . We are looking after him so well. Be it milk, food or medicines—everything by the hour, right on time. But none of it matters to this man!'

As Pramila's voice rose, Narmada felt increasingly ill at ease fearing *Chikkappa* might overhear their conversation. Pramila seemed to pride herself in caring for the old man with what she considered as exemplary conscientious, and her pride stridently came through as she held forth. In a way, she was right. There was no cause for complaint: *Chikkappa*'s room was airy and well-lit, his bed was covered with clean white sheet; on a stool within his easy reach stood a jug of water, a tumbler, a pocket radio and a calling bell; a big clock hung on the wall; nurses from a nearby nursing home came at regular intervals to change his sheets and to give him sponge bath; coffee, meals and snacks were served from time to time; and a doctor came twice a day to examine him—no wonder all those visiting were full of praise for such meticulous arrangements.

Surveying the scene, a question bothered Narmada—can physical comforts alone keep a man happy and contended even if he was living his last days? Just then, Appanna, who saw her approaching him, accompanied by Pramila, motioned to her to sit on a chair nearby his bed. Pramila left her at the door—presumably because it was not the 'appointed hour'.

Appanna was lying on the bed stiffly, looking like an effigy made of bamboo sticks. Narmada, sitting beside him, racked her brains for the right words to say to him. Suddenly remembering, she said, 'I am going home next week. The children have their holidays.'

He began to say in a dry voice, 'Going home, child? . . . Jalaja . . . .' but a fit of coughing interrupted him. His speech failing him due to continued and severe coughing, he tried to convey something to her by gesturing wildly with his hands. 'This cough will be the end of me,' was all that he managed to say, or what she could hear.

Just before leaving for the hometown, Narmada had gone to see Latthi in Mysore where she lived now.

Their meandering talk had turned to Appanna-*Chikkappa*. When Latthi had visited him last, it seemed he was complaining about his lower back being weary due to constant lying in the bed, and it had struck her, remembering the past, that if Jalaja were to be there, she would have lovingly massaged his weary back to afford him some comfort.

'*Chikki* there and *Chikkappa* here . . . .' Latthi had sighed, before she asked, 'What do you think, Nammu?

'*Chikkappa* looked as if he has been orphaned when I saw him lying in bed, all alone in that room. Of course, Keshava looks after him well. Everything is fine. Even Pramila is all right. She has made very good arrangements. But . . .'

Latthi had continued, as if echoing what was on Narmada's mind, 'They had never lived apart even for a day, you know. But now . . . when he is at the end of his life . . . ? . . . When I think of it, I don't think even a true married couple could have been so much in love.'

She had then asked Narmada, 'do you remember . . . . ?', and it was the beginning of a long conversation that came alive with events and feelings of the time they had spent in their childhood with Jalaja and Appanna in that House of Pillars.

It was from then on that Narmada's resolve to go to *Chikki*'s house had become increasingly strong. So much so that the very next day after landing in her parents' house, she had set off with her children to Jalaja-*Chikki*'s house.

With the hem of her sari hitched up, Jalaja was dragging a dry coconut frond just after dislodging it from a bush on which it had fallen, and when she saw Narmada with her kids approaching her, she dropped the frond from her hand, unhitched the sari's folds and stood waiting for the visitors.

Jalaja, furrowing her forehead and peering with narrowed eyes, enquired, 'Who . . . Nammu?' as Narmada neared her.

Narmada noticed that Jalaja-*Chikki* had become very thin and frail, and she answered, 'Yes *Chikki*, it is me.'

As she surveyed the surroundings, Narmada recognized the familiar sights of yester years like the *tulsi* plant within its bricked square, the jasmine-creeper that embraced the *parijatha* tree and the towering *pairi*-mango tree that dominated the whole space with its majestic spread. Just as these came into her view, her childhood memories came rushing back to her. Happiness of a little girl spread on her face as she remembered the thrill of sitting in a swing tied to the branch of that familiar tree, going up higher and higher in the air in heady competition with other children and the wind blowing in her face.

'Come on in, child. I am happy you felt at all like seeing this *Chikki*.' said Jalaja. Narmada and her children followed her into the house and then to the kitchen.

It was the same endearing smile, the same rush of words. 'Are these your children? What are their names? What will you have . . . Wait, I think I'll give you some warm milk.'

She placed a vessel on the hearth with milk, and pushed in the embers and firewood into the hearth. She took some cookies from the cookie tin and put them in a plate for the children.

'Children, come, eat,' she said. 'And how fast they have grown . . . ! I think the last I saw your son was at his naming ceremony—Is that right? Your visit is always short . . . just for a few days, and then you just can't meet everyone in that limited time. . . . Wait, children . . . . I'll give milk to drink . . . . and then I'll take you to see the cattle in the shed.'

She still could instinctively feel the heart beats of children.

As the children were having their milk, she told them to be careful while going to the cattle—shed or moving around in the compound—'have an eye on the ground and walk cautiously' she said, and as a cautionary tale, she told them how Narmada had once jumped off a ledge and broken her tooth.

'What memory!' Narmada said to herself.

Taking them to the cattle-shed she quickly showed the children how to feed hay to the cows—a few strands at a time, and she then rushed back to the kitchen with Narmada in tow.

'No hurry, right, Nammu? You must eat here before leaving. I'll set water for cooking rice. Just wait for a moment. It's going to be a simple meal . . . with, of course, your favourite chutney of boiled raw mango' she went on.

Narmada was touched that Jalaja-*Chikki* actually remembered her favourite dish after so many years . . . and was now hastening to make it for her with such eagerness. The bitter irony, it occurred to her, was that a monumental effort had been underway for years to put up a barrier against this mighty flood of love.

Narmada was suddenly overcome with emotions and was unable to utter any word, as if her throat had got stuck. She kept quiet, fearing she might burst out crying if she tried to speak.

Jalaja-*Chikki* made Narmada sit on a low stool in the kitchen, as she went about cooking.

'I had been to Keshava's house.' At last, the words formed.

Chikki's hand that was busy stirring the pot with a ladle became still.

Resting the ladle across the lid of the pot, she asked, turning towards Narmada, 'How is your *Chikkappa*, Nammu?' and waited as if her entire existence had turned into a question. Her expectant gaze seemed to search the very depths of Narmada's eyes.

'He is bedridden,' Narmada almost choked on the words.

Jalaja-*Chikki*, bent her head pretending to stoke the fire.

'This is the problem with raw firewood,' she muttered. 'There's always more smoke than fire.'

Blaming the non-existent smoke, she turned aside and wiped her eyes with the end of her sari, as the flames leapt up in the hearth.

The excuse of the smoke brought tears to Narmada's eyes too, as she got up from the low stool.

Narmada left the kitchen and wandered through the house where she had once played and run all over. The old house hadn't changed much and looked the same, except that at some places it had become dilapidated. Narmada felt sad when she saw the bases of the large pillars which were so much a part of her familiarity with *Chikki*'s house had partly sunk into the floor. The bamboo poles placed around them to supplement the pillars also looked weak and seemed to totter. She was alarmed to find that the roof of the porch at the back of the house had come down precariously low.

By the time Narmada and her children came back to the kitchen, food was waiting for them. Jalaja-*Chikki* sat down to eat only after the rest had finished. She was up in no time and began to fuss around.

'You didn't eat anything at all!' Narmada scolded her aunt gently.

'I don't get hungry these days, Nammu. As you can see, I have aged.' she said.

With the preamble, 'After your *Chikkappa* left for Bangalore . . .' Jalaja went on to explain how, feeling lost and benumbed, she couldn't normally bring herself to cook. She said there was no certainty if she would even eat on any given day, sometimes managing with just flattened rice mixed with curd, and then went on to explain that she cooked that day only because Narmada and her children had stayed for lunch.

Referring to the breadfruit-curry that she had made that day for them, she said, 'Your *Chikkappa* used to love bead-fruit.'

Then, with great earnestness, she asked Narmada, 'Shall I give you some breadfruit to carry to Bangalore?'

Narmada swallowed hard. No solid food—not even a grain of rice, so to say—had gone down *Chikkappa*'s gullet in the last several months.

'Forget it, child. I'm crazy!' *Chikki* checked herself.

When Narmada was readying to leave in the evening, Jalaja-*Chikki* quickly picked some jasmines from the creeper in the backyard, strung them up and pinned them to Narmada's plait.

After Narmada had bid goodbye and was almost on the road, Jalaja-*Chikki* called out to her from behind, 'Narmada, wait for a minute' and catching up with her in a great rush, she began, 'Tell *Chikkappa* . . . .', and then fell silent holding Narmada's hand and gazing at her face.

Narmada's eyes could sense that words came right up to *Chikki's* lips and played on them without getting uttered.

'All right . . . you now go . . .' said Jalaja in a tone of having said a lot before concluding.

Jalaja-*Chikki* had let go of Narmada's hand only after she had gone a couple of steps.

Narmada once again had a message to carry,—to Bangalore this time. But that made her wonder—what message did Jalaja-*Chikki*' give anyway? And at that instant, she also tried to remember—Did I even deliver *Chikkappa's* message to *Chikki*, after all?